SNIPS AND SNAILS

Katherine Clare

What are littleboys made of?
Snips and snails,
And puppy-dogs' tails,
That's what little boys are made of

UNKNOWN

CHAPTER 1

"So...?" asks the small, fabulously glossy dark haired, heavily pregnant woman who is my best friend in the world.

We are in her large kitchen, I'm seated at a fashionably distressed cream wooden island. My dear friend Fiona potters about by an enormous yellow Aga amid a myriad granite worktops. The chaotic order of this warm family home in which I spend so much time always makes me happy. Pot plants, candles, quirky clay vessels and antique glass vases adorn each surface. I notice the new Joe Wicks cookbook on a swirly cast iron stand is open on the same page as it was the last time I was here. And the time before that.

Fiona's chin dips and her chocolate brown eyes widen with intrigue.

"Well I've joined a dating site and a few guys have messaged me" I answer.

I feel myself blush under Fiona's excited look.

"A couple of them seem quite nice" I say. I unlock my phone with an old land line number I had years ago, the only series of numbers I can successfully call to mind and show her the pictures of two guys I've earmarked as favourites.

Pete, 38, tall, Mediterranean looking. Several photos show him on holiday skiing, raising a glass on what appears to be a boat, and one of him clapping enthusiastically while standing in the audience of a theatre. The write up underneath states that he loves travelling the world – great, has an interest in cricket – not so great, and rather disconcertingly 'no time wasters please'.

The other guy, Tom 40, has only one photo, obviously a selfie, showing gorgeous teal eyes with silky caramel hair flopping into them. A la Hugh Grant in *'Four Weddings and a Funeral'*. A small paragraph underneath says he loves wildlife and walking in the countryside, and has been single for four months.

"Oh he looks lovely!" squeals Fiona, "look he doesn't smoke and rarely drinks and he's got a young son like you!"

As she puts her arm around me, I hug her back, only half dreading that now the prospect of finding me a suitable life partner may well become her new project.

The sound of the heavy front door being unlocked is followed by the cheerful energy of Fiona's husband John arriving home. Tall, fair haired, with circular metal glasses and today wearing a tweed jacket in mixed shades of green. With his slightly effeminate voice and mannerisms, and flamboyant style, one might assume he was gay. But a stronger, more genuine union than Fiona and John have would be hard to come by.

"Hi!" John choruses as he enters the kitchen. "How are my two girls?" his deep regard for his wife evident in the warm smile he gives her as he kisses her cheek. The two girls are Fiona and the baby girl who is due to be born in March. The new parents are pretty much certain now that her name will be Tamsin Stephanie.

"Bethan's online dating now" Fiona informs John delightedly.

"Oh, joined the dark side have we?" John says (I think, not for the first time as though a parrot or minor bird might).

"Well Darth Vader's a working single parent so I might well do that" I laugh. "I'm actually meeting one of them, Tom tomorrow evening". I feel my blush deepening to somewhere in the region of dark beetroot as John and Fiona grin at me like particularly gleeful Cheshire cats. "Dylan's staying over at Oliver's anyway so I thought, why not?" I shrug.

"Where are you meeting him?" asks John, a look of concern shadowing the excitement of a moment ago. I tell him we've arranged to meet at seven at The Blacksmith's Arms in town.

"Well make sure you have your phone with you fully charged if you need to call us OK?" John tells me, and I feel touched to have such caring friends.

"I definitely will, thanks John" I reply as I reach for my bag, scarf and coat. "Dylan will be just about finishing karate now so I'd better get going."

I hug both Fiona and John as I make my way through their kitchen, into their elegant hallway. A lamp with the base in the shape of a stag sits atop a cream console table, along with a bronze leaf shaped key dish. A large rococo style mirror opposite reveals a corner of the lounge in which a large Christmas tree still stands.

"Any problems at all, if it's awkward and you need rescuing, call OK?" says John as the three of us reach the front door.

"Oh you'll have a brilliant time" smiles Fiona.

I thank them, tell them I'll see them soon, and head outside.

***

I love our maisonette. It always gladdens my heart to be here. As I move around the kitchen area preparing dinner for my ten year old son Dylan, I can't help but smile. I watch my sweet natured, kind son playing on his tablet at the mango wood table in the dining half of the room.

I go over and kiss his head, he is completely engrossed in what looks like building a town.

"Dinner will be ready in a minute sweetheart" I tell him.

A large pile of assessment forms I need to look over sit on the table. I'm a children and young people's therapy assistant. For two years now I've been working as a guidance counsellor at Cranwell Gate Secondary School. Helping to safeguard children from peer pressure, volatile situations, and often their own thoughts can be challenging but it's all I've ever wanted to do.

As a child, I lived with my mum, Shirley. I always felt Mum loved me dearly, but she suffered with what we now know to be major depressive disorder. Undiagnosed and thus unmedicated, Mum struggled to cope with a child and on three occasions I spent time at St Anne's children's home in our town.

The home closed down over twelve years ago now, but the building still stands, a forlorn reminder of the help we were given when Mum was at her very lowest. Though I was always warmly welcomed and found all the adults there warm, polite and kind, it must have been excruciating for my poor mum. I feel compelled to cuddle Dylan and I put my arms around his shoulders.

"You alright Mum?" Dylan asks matter of factly, such a reasonable, balanced soul even at ten.

I smile and ruffle his chestnut hair, "totally" I tell him.

CHAPTER 2

There it is again. I knew it would come. My heart beating louder, faster. Is it still in there? I'm not sure. I wish I had some socks on, it's been raining today and the grass is all muddy and squelchy. I wonder how long it'll be for this time. I peer hopefully in the glass door. Yelling, shouting, that's all I hear. She won't let me in. He won't let her let me in. It starts to rain again. My legs hurt. My back does too. Will I die in the night? I hope so.

CHAPTER 3

Though I don't work on Tuesdays, there's usually paperwork I've accrued throughout the week which I like to get done at home on Tuesday afternoons. I find it sometimes helps to construct assessments of students when I am at home, as I can think more objectively.

Today however, I didn't have any so I have invited my mum over, and have just been tidying round beforehand. I'm aware there are signs of OCD in my home, for which I routinely receive well meaning, yet unsolicited critique from friends. I suppose it's a habit I've developed. I don't have cleaning rituals or anything, I just find I feel calmer if my things are exactly as I like them.

I'm glad to be spending this time with Mum as I worry about her. Her close friend Keith died last year. I really miss him too, he was like a father figure and friend, always quick to smile and easy to talk to.

I bring two mugs of coffee over to the table where Mum sits, looking out of the large picture window opposite.

"Nice to see a song thrush in your garden" she muses.

It warms my heart to see her taking pleasure from little things in the world. Proper treatment for depression has enabled my sweet, unassuming mum to rediscover life and show it what she has to give, but was unable to for so long. It really is like watching a rose coming into bloom now that we live in a time where serious mental health conditions are much more understood.

"I've got a date with a fella' tonight Mum" I say both gently and consiprationally.

"Oh what's he like?" mum asks with a childish delight.

"Well I've met him online, so not actually in real life yet. But as far as I can tell, he seems nice."

"Well be careful, and see if he's got an older brother!" mum glows with mirth.

"Easy tiger!" I laugh as I pull her into a hug.

Just before 5pm there is an eager, childish sounding knock at the door. I run downstairs in the old jumper, tracksuit bottoms and socks I'm wearing and answer it. Dylan's friend Oliver and his mum Emma stand on the doorstep smiling broadly.

"Hi" I greet them, "Come in. Dylan's just grabbing a couple of things he wants to bring. Thanks so much for having him over."

Dylan comes bounding down the stairs carrying a Sainsbury's bag containing his tablet, charger and various other things from his room.

I fetch his coat from the kitchen. "Be good, miss you darling" I say as I help him into it. Emma and I share a warm smile as our two boys tare away excitedly to her car.

The house always misses Dylan when he's not here. It sort of releases an empty energy. I'm glad he's made such good friends though who, as an only child, he can spend time away from school with.

A rush of excitement courses through me. For the first time in years, I have a date to to get ready for.

In the kitchen, I pour myself two thirds of a glass of Chablis and assemble a small plate of buttered crackers. I want to take the edge off my slight nervousness, and I don't want my stomach rumbling on the date.

I hurry upstairs with my little feast. I select a music channel on the TV in my bedroom – *Magic*, some mellow background music to help calm me a bit, and set about making myself date ready.

On top of my everyday make-up from earlier, I give my brown eyes a smokey look with dark grey eyeshadow and several coats of black mascara. After sweeping shimmery apricot blusher onto my cheeks, I run a warm bath. I always apply my make up before having a bath, its just the order in which I've always done it. I add a small amount of lavender bath foam, I want to feel relaxed, but not to fall asleep.

After my bath, I return to the bedroom to dry my hair. Spritzing a little perfume onto my wrists and neck heightens the sense of adventure further. Its an expensive one, Coco Mademoiselle, which I hardly ever wear.

After cleaning my teeth, I apply a nude lip gloss. I select black slim leg jeans, black ankle boots with a mid heel, and a glittery emerald top. Looking in the mirror by my wardrobe, I don't feel totally comfortable in the top. I lost two stone last year, and it fits perfectly, it just somehow seems too gaudy. I swap it for a smart peach jumper and feel much more myself.

Downstairs I turn off all the lights except the one for the entrance hall. Grabbing my everyday winter coat and shoulder bag from the kitchen, I leave the house.

CHAPTER 4

You were so easy to find. Too easy. Stupid like most people. To stupid to realise that putting where you live, work, the morons you're closest friends with, and pictures of where you go on Facebook isn't always a good idea. Consumed only with the notion of bragging to your banal friends about some shallow achievement which means absolutely nothing in the scheme of things.

Why haven't you moved away from this dump? How can you be happy here?

CHAPTER 5

The Blacksmith's Arms is an architecturally stunning building, seventeenth century cream coloured walls meeting a dramatic thatched roof.

Despite not really being somebody who enjoys pubs, as I don't like crowds, I've been here a couple of times before and on each occasion felt at home.

The interior is warmly lit and low ceilinged. An ancient brick fireplace with a crackling fire is ensconced between walls of dark shipyard wood. By the fire place are two maroon leather, Queen Anne style chairs, and sitting in one, I recognise immediately, is Tom.

"Hi, I'm Bethan" I say as I walk over.

"Hi Bethan, Tom" his demeanour quickly puts me at ease. He rises to hug me and, shallow as it sounds, I'm relieved to see he's taller than me (at five foot nine, that's not a regular occurrence).

"What would you like to drink?" Tom asks me and I reply that I'd love a small white wine. As his smiling, seemingly self assured form heads towards the bar, I am suddenly filled with a slight trepidation.

As a result of concentrating on my work, Dylan, and ostensibly working with children, I'm so unused to meeting new people and it occurs to me that I may not be very natural at it. But I quickly find Tom very easy to talk to. A combination of the wine, his comfortable manner, and the warmth of the fireplace allow me to feel incredibly relaxed, almost blissful.

"What sort of music are you into?" Tom asks me and I'm drawn to his intense bluey green eyes and realise that I find him staggeringly attractive. I feel a little overwhelmed so I imagine he's a teacher at the school or a parent of one of my students.

"I love music" I say, loving him for gently nodding encouragement. "I love classic rock best, but also songs I grew up with that were in the charts in the early nineties."

Having this handsome, charismatic man making me the focus of his attention isn't making me feel horribly self conscious, it actually makes me feel really desirable.

As the evening unfolds, I consider how lucky I am that there obviously are really nice guys out there who seem to find me attractive too. This concept really lifts my confidence and I feel uncharacteristically emboldened.

"They do really nice food here" I hear myself saying in a confident voice "Shall we have a meal?" I love that I can naturally talk to a relative stranger as though he were an old friend. It's true, the more you practice things, the easier they become.

"That would be lovely" Tom replies, his gaze smiling, and together we head into the dining area of the pub.

A low beamed doorway leads into a dining room intimately lit with the glow of tea lights on each table. Tom and I sit near the back of the room, by another fire, perhaps to resume the magic of before. It's glorious for me to eat out on any occasion as I usually make quick meals for Dylan and I and my mouth waters at the thought of flavours, herbs and spices I wouldn't generally have.

Tom orders the lamb shank and I the seafood linguine. After the waitress (who's slimmer than me and with amazing hair, but Tom doesn't look at once) has taken away our empty plates, we sit in agreeable silence, gazing at one another. I reach over and take Tom's hands in mine. They engulf mine, and as I feel their warmth and slight roughness, I am totally at ease.

Tom's ocean coloured eyes are mesmerising in the candle light.

We talk effortlessly about anything and everything, from adverts we remembered as kids, to the political situation of the UK.

Tom and I leave the pub. The evening is slightly chilly and the black night sky with its gold stars has thrown its cloak over the day. I tell Tom that I only live two minutes away, but he insists on walking me home.

Wending through the familiar streets with Tom, I hadn't been aware that I missed such comfortable companionship. Now I realise, I must on some level, have yearned for it. I look down and see we are holding hands. I squeeze Tom's hand, which he reciprocates with a warm smile. Tom's one of those people who don't only smile with their mouth. Their whole being seems to ignite.

When we turn the corner into my road, which happens far quicker than I would have liked it to, I tell Tom "This is me, thank you so much for a wonderful evening. I'm so glad I met you." I reach up and hug him.

"It was brilliant. Get yourself in, it's cold. Night night sweetheart" he says smiling at me.

I feel so protected and I have to stop myself skipping up the steps like Little Red Riding Hood.

Inside, I take off my boots and coat and make a cup of tea. I take the tea up to my bedroom. After wiping my face with baby wipes and cleaning my teeth, I slip into bed. I can't sleep as I'm sizzling with excitement, so I try and watch TV. But my mind is full of what a superb time I had and how vibrant Tom made me feel.

CHAPTER 6

I wake, for the first time in a while feeling really well rested. Emma said she'd bring Dylan back at around ten, so I have over an hour and a half to myself. I sigh as I snuggle into the duvet, the thought of an empty Saturday stretching before me. I think fondly of the date last night. I really like Tom. The conversation between us flowed effortlessly, we have things in common and a similar sense of humour. Plus I can't deny I'm very attracted to him. He had a way of making me feel really secure, both in myself and with the world around me. I'd definitely like to see him again. I don't worry that he might not call either, as I sense somehow that he will.

It's probably a good idea to put a wash on now, and maybe get some ironing done from the previous one. Dylan always seems to have football gear in need of a clean. I slowly get out of bed and head downstairs. I can hear a tinny sounding tune like something computerised which I'm not sure is coming from next door's or not. It takes me a moment to realise that it is the sound of my phone ringing. I must have left it on the table last night when I came in and forgotten to take it up to bed with me.

I reach the table at exactly the moment when the call rings off. It's probably a company calling about feedback or changing my broadband provider. It then hits me, I hope Fiona's OK, or Dylan, or Emma.

But when I scroll to recent calls I see that it was Tom. I smile, I feel lighter and somehow taller that I have a man who is so interested in talking to me. I notice then that there is a number five in brackets next to his name and that he has tried to call me five times this morning. Did he forget something? He walked me home but he didn't come in, he couldn't have left anything here. I'll call him back in a moment when I've gathered my thoughts.

I turn on the coffee machine Fiona and John bought me for my birthday and whilst it's working it's wizardry I open the back door into the utility area to collect the washing basket. Coming back into the kitchen area, I begin amassing things we'll need for the week. Dylan's spare school jumper, a couple of tops I like to wear to work, when I hear my phone ring again.

I see that it is Tom and press accept. I remember when I was a receptionist in a hotel years ago they said to always say 'hello' with a smile as it will lift your voice on the phone. It really works as I find I'm smiling naturally and can hear the excitement in my voice.

"Hi Tom, sorry I missed your calls, my phone was downstairs. Are you OK?"

"Hi Bethan" the relief in Tom's voice is palpable. "Not ignoring me are you?" he laughs good naturedly and is at once the engaging man of last night.

"I just wondered if you fancied grabbing a coffee?

"What now?" I stumble, slightly wrong footed, whatever I was expecting him to say, it wasn't this. I quickly compose myself and think of the lovely evening we shared previously and how I'd very much like to feel again as I did then.

"I can't today, Dylan will be back from his friend's house soon and I'd like to hang out with him and watch a film. I'd love to see you again soon though" I say.

"Oh right. Well which day could you do this week?" he asks.

I sense a tiny fraction of discontent running through his otherwise animated voice. I quickly dismiss this as simply him wanting to spend time with me sooner and I smile with the feathery brush of flattery.

"I can probably be free on Tuesday evening, I could get my mum to have Dylan for a couple of hours."

I say this casually as I haven't obviously asked mum yet. Also, I don't want Dylan to always stay over at another person's house because I'm dating and trying to meet someone special. His home is here with me and I think its important that anyone I date knows from the beginning that I may only be free for a couple of hours some evenings because of this.

We arrange to meet up on Tuesday at six in The Blacksmith's Arms again, and I look forward to another date with the enigmatic Tom. Only a very slight part of me registering something close to alarm.

Fiona carefully lowers herself onto her olive green velvet sofa.

"That's not normal though is it? Calling five times the next morning to arrange another date?"

I sip my tea on the matching sofa opposite.

"But we had so much in common, I loved it that he held my hand and that we were laughing together. I don't want to write him off because he's a bit too insistent. Who knows how I come across? There's so much about him I really like Fi."

"Bless you, you always see the best in people. OK but explain to him that his enthusiasm can be quite demanding. Imagine if you called a man five times the next morning? You wouldn't see him for dust and would be labelled a bunny boiler, but when men are too pushy it's just them asserting their valour. Pisses me off!"

We both throw back our heads in heartfelt laughter.

CHAPTER 7

Monday and Tuesday pass by smoothly. Dylan's getting on really well at Corn Meadows Primary in year five, and he loves his teacher Mr Miller.

I watch fondly as my sweet son sits at the table drawing. He's so talented at creating cartoon characters, monsters with super powers and portraits of his friends. He wants to be an artist when he grows up.

As I potter around the kitchen area I think about Tom. How wonderful it was to be in his company, feeling alive from his energy. So what if he was a touch pushy? It means I don't have to go through the motions of feeling anxious that he hasn't called and did he not find me attractive? Was I boring, silly or awkward? I feel utterly accepted for me and perhaps I wasn't expecting that.

Dylan's father David and I met at uni. We tried to make things work, or rather I tried to. I lost count of how many other girls he was sleeping with. I can honestly say, I've never felt the need for another adult in my life with Dylan. Together we're a team and I have my Mum, really good friends, and a house and job I love.

The tinkle of the door bell peals through my musings. It'll be mum, come to pick up Dylan.

"That'll be Nan sweetheart" I tell him. "Get your coat on."

Dylan puts on his navy padded jacket. "Can I take my art stuff Mum?" he asks earnestly.

"Of course you can darling" I reply, giving him a quick cuddle.

My mum is looking happy. She loves her garden and tells me she has been potting some tulip bulbs for the summer.

"I hope they turn out as they were on the packet – marbled" she says.

"What could you do if they didn't?" I genuinely wonder at this for a second, then say
"Thanks so much for having Dylan, I'll pick him up at around quarter to nine."

"I get to spend time with my lovely grandson" beams mum.

The two people I love most in the world leave the house chatting. I hum to myself as I make my way upstairs. I put on a nineties music channel, and tie my hair back. I'm going to go a bit heavier with my make-up tonight. I think the candlelight in The Blacksmith's Arms will lend itself to it. Also, I somehow feel sexier in myself. I go for a rich plum lipstick which I'm pleased to see makes my lips appear much fuller. I don't often wear eyeliner and when I go to open the one black one I own, I notice that it's a bit clumpy from non-use. I wipe the end of the wand on the lip of the tube and apply a glossy dark ring to each of my eyes, flicking upwards at the edges.

I have a nice collection of stud earrings which I wear to work, though for this evening, I decide to adorn my lobes with the sparkly diamanté drop earrings my friend Amy bought me. I smile as I picture them twinkling in the flickering candlelight.

Just then, my phone rings. I look at it and see that it's Tom calling. I feel slight disappointment if he's phoning to cancel, or if he'll be late as we won't then have as much time together. At least he's letting me know though. I can always catch up on a couple of episodes of *Luther* I've missed.

"Hi Tom, everything OK?" I ask hopefully.

"Hiya, you're still coming yes?" His reply confuses me slightly. Is he joking perhaps? Everyone likes to think they're hilarious don't they so maybe he's one of those people with quite a dead-pan sense of humour, which I quite like. Though the impression I've formed so far of Tom and casual joviality don't particularly seem to correlate.

"Yes, I'm just getting ready now. Really looking forward to seeing you again."

"OK. See you at six then." And the next sound I hear is a dead line. No goodbye. A little part of me feels somewhat disconcerted but the larger part of me, which is excited to be with Tom again quickly diminishes the first.

Everybody is different and expresses themselves according to their individual idiosyncrasies and quirks, and of course, their experiences beforehand. Maybe he was let down by someone in the past and so checking I won't do the same actually seems perfectly reasonable.

I opt for a black loose tunic, tights, and the mid- heeled ankle boots I wore before. I felt just the right height in them next to Tom. Impulsively, I then fasten the fine silver chain with heart pendant around my neck which Keith bought me before he passed away.

I once read in *Vogue* in a doctor's waiting room that the effortlessly stylish Coco Chanel used to say that the way to be perfectly accessorized is to remove the last thing you put on. But touching the necklace with the heart pendant sitting at my throat, I just don't have the heart to do so. Keith bought it for my birthday a couple of years ago and had the underside engraved with 'Dearest Daughter'. It meant so much to him to present me with it, and I feel a swell of emotion for what a kind-hearted, thoughtful person he was.

It abruptly occurs to me that if I were suddenly sick now, or something arose with Mum or Dylan, would Tom be angry with me? That dear man last week wouldn't have been, now I'm not so sure.

It's one of those mid January evenings which stays brighter, but has a chill wind. It may have been an idea to put my hair up into a loose, boho style bun. Though on second thoughts I'm glad I didn't do so as I tend to blush a lot when I'm a little excitable, and like to have my hair around me. I had it cut just before Christmas and I enjoy the way it falls now. (Though not when being blown from all directions by the wind obviously).

I head down St Henry's Road and then turn left onto the high street where The Blacksmith's Arms stands, as it has for centuries. Though not always opposite a Sainsbury's Local I think while chuckling to myself.

There are only a couple of cars parked outside the pub this evening, one of those Smart Cars which I've never seen in moss green before, and a black BMW. It must be a quiet evening. I'm glad as I want to gaze into Tom's eyes, not joust for a place to stand amid a frenzy of football fans, there to watch a game. The only sporting event I usually tune into is Wimbledon with my mum as she loves it.

I enter the pub through the main entrance, a welcome warmth immediately enveloping me. I smile as I see Tom sitting on a stool at the bar. He comes over and hugs me with a kind of firm tenderness and I instantly sense the affable soul from before.

"You OK hun?" he says, kissing me on the cheek.

"Yes, fine thanks" I answer, "How about you?"

Tom replies warmly that he is very well and asks me if I'd like a white wine.

"Could I have a Diet Coke please? I'm collecting Dylan later from his Nan's."

"Oh. OK." A faint trace of what looks like displeasure moves across Tom's eyes but is then replaced in a flash by an affectionate twinkle.

Tom has four beers before our meal arrives. I've noticed he does tend to drink quite a lot. However, this is only the second time I've ever met him, he may be nervous and some people have a tremendous capacity for alcohol.

"How was your day?" I ask, reaching to lightly caress his upper arm.

"Good" Tom nods. He speaks animatedly about his career in which he is clearly very confident, though I don't really understand what it is he actually does.

Something in Tom's energy seems to have shifted tonight. In place of the previous vigour I experienced with him, is an icy tickle of foreboding.

I am enjoying my choice of meal – the Dover sole in lemon butter with new potatoes. It's salty but pleasantly so. I ponder which herb it is I can taste. It's not sage, I don't think its rosemary. I'm not entirely sure what oregano tastes like.

"Why are you wearing that?" Tom asks, cutting through my thoughts and pulling me back into the moment. He nods his head to indicate my neck area. His briny eyes sparkling with menace, as the rest of his being seems to blunt, as though they were drinking its life blood.

"This tunic?" I reply, feeling confronted without knowing why. It's not low cut or see through.

"No that necklace, I don't want you wearing stuff like that any more."

"Why?" I hear a confused, thin voice distantly related to mine answer.

"Why?" Tom feigns a nasty laugh as if I already know the answer. "The reason all women wear necklaces, so men will look at their breasts. And why have you plastered your face in all that shit? Do you want blokes to fancy you?" He snorts derisively.

Time stands still. I'm genuinely discombobulated. Will he burst out laughing and exclaim "I was only joking, your face was a picture" and I'd have to then bear in mind that he has a slightly disturbing sense of humour?

But he doesn't. The intense aqua stare just watches me accusingly.

His naturally commanding presence, which before made me feel so protected, suddenly gives me the sensation of being in some kind of parallel universe. Removed from the safety of familiarity.

I surprise myself by how calm my reaction is. I cross my knife and fork on my plate, then reach into my bag for my purse. I remove two twenty pound notes and place them on the table. This is much more than the meal will cost but it is I feel, a necessary manoeuvrer. I take a steadying breath into my chest and formulate my reply.

"I work with young people and children, helping them with their confidence. I may not be brimming over with self esteem, but I've enough not to put up with someone telling me what to wear. Please don't call me again."

"At Cranwell Gate Secondary School, for three years this June." A nasty smirk taints the features I wanted so very much to kiss only days ago.

I don't recall volunteering this information, though on our last date I did have more to drink than I usually would. I am however, fully aware of his tactic, attempting to wrong foot me and cause me to doubt myself.

I leave the pub, my heart walloping within my chest cavity. My teeth are pressed tightly together and my hands are shaking. The juxtaposition of when I last walked on the high street, so full of excitement taunting me. I turn right onto St Henry's road. Though it's not cold, I can feel myself shivering.

I reach my house, my breath exiting my body loudly. For the sake of expediency, I retrieve the spare key from my coat pocket, opting not to fumble for the main one in my bag. The outdoor light illuminates the front door. Unlocking it with a trembling hand, I fall into the sanctity of my home.

CHAPTER 8

I've been working on some student files in the library this morning. It's so peaceful in here, it's recently been renovated and is fresh and modern. My mind is starting to wander a bit now, I didn't sleep very well last night. It'll be lunch time soon and I'll get a strong coffee. I start to think about the warped ideas of love people can have. How they can see it as an object to jealously posses, tightly, with both hands, to control obsessively, or to experiment with cruelly.

Like the child who takes care of a rabbit, feeding and nurturing it. But not allowing it to scamper around the lawn as it might run away and leave the protector. Cuddling it so tightly, the little thing becomes crushed as it wasn't afforded the room it needed to grow, to live.

Like the Victorian lady who pins a butterfly, loving it's beauty. All can marvel at such beauty for evermore, though it can never again spread its wings.

Things in nature cannot be dominated or they'll die. Or develop a distorted co- dependency on their tormentor as dogs who are abused sadly often do. We will die too, sometimes literally. Though at other times only our souls will die and we'll still walk around existing.

When I trained I worked with adult victims of abusive relationships, men and women. The dark side of human nature being the indiscriminate creature it is, I saw people from all walks of life. Though all wearing differing shades of the same countenance. The one which says that the part of their brain that tells their heart to pump blood and their eyes to blink still functions, but the part that registers hurt, not so. Like a closed down fairground ride, it has rusted with non-use.

I've seen victims excuse, and often even protect their abusers. That's one of the reasons I wanted to study psychology. Helping people to realise that many people mistake the idea of forgiveness. Forgiving someone doesn't mean condoning their poor behaviour, but to draw a line under it so as you can move on.

For my job, I have read extensively about controlling behaviour. The concept of systematic coercive, or controlling behaviour, bullying, degrading and humiliating a person has now been recognised as being as much part of domestic abuse as physical and sexual violence. As a result, Coercive or controlling behaviour offence has just become law in the UK.

It's a movement happening now which in a miniscule way, I too am trying to champion with my work. Knowing how controlling behaviour can occur, and seeing it in someone else, is very different from recognising it in your own life. I find I'm actually struggling to separate the threads of different memories of Tom which are woven together. I just can't understand why he'd change so quickly like that?

He must know I wouldn't then still be interested? I thought he was looking for a relationship? OK that may not be with me, but he didn't need to be so horrible to me on a date HE was really keen to arrange? Doesn't make sense.

Well it's one thing to see the good in people and in human nature, but another to excuse behaviour which makes you feel really uncomfortable and the disregard with which he spoke to me is inexcusable. I would advise my students against entering into a friendship or relationship of any kind with some one like that. Somebody who enjoys power games.

Much as I liked Tom before, I know that it's imperative that I realise now how degrading he can be and move on. Not to adapt so that that becomes normal and acceptable. It's scarily easy to brainwash a person or group of people -just watch a documentary on cults. Oh well, you live and learn, who ever said human beings made decisions based on logic? I'll be a bit more cautious next time.

"Hi Miss Archer" a blue eyed girl with long, dark hair smiles at me as she approaches the computer area.

"Hi Lucy" I smile back. I have never worked with Lucy in my position as a therapy assistant but she is one of many children I know from around the school. Lucy sits down quietly and logs onto a computer.

I look over and see Matthew Lyndon. He seems to spend a lot of time here on his own reading. I hope he's OK and not feeling ostracised from other kids. Maybe he just likes his own company and loves reading, and so I decide against going over and asking if he's alright.

I look at the notes I've made for Marcia Hodge's file. I worry about her. Saddens me deeply to see gifted youngsters misdirecting all their energy into what they think will make them acceptable to overbearing parents (who they've yet to realise are as broken as they are) their peers, (who one day may realise were as lonely as they were) or themselves, who I just hope will realise they are wonderful and unique, with so much to give.

Outwardly, Marcia seems popular and happy, I know of her parents and her younger brother Rhys. But I need to help the Marcia I see realise why she has been self harming, cutting her arm with a pair of compasses or chafing it with a rock.

So deep was I in thought that I must have missed the bell signifying lunchtime. Sometimes I have a meal in the canteen, though today I've bough a tomato and basil pasta salad from Sainsbury's which I'll eat in the staffroom. Its more subdued in there than the rowdiness of the canteen and I may well catch my friend Amy Croft, who teaches English and drama. I collect together my files and notes, and put them into my bag. I then head to the staff room.

I'm in luck. The staff room is peace itself, it's pale blue carpet free from the footfall of busy, harassed teachers. It has wide windows looking out onto a garden and picnic area which the youngsters use in the summer. In the far left hand corner, is a sink and small kitchenette area. By the microwave, stands my dear friend Amy.

She turns as I open the door, "Hey Bethan" she grins, coming over to hug me.

Amy has that small-boned, delicate femininity one envisages all men wanting to do battle to shield.
With hair the colour of dark honey, cut into a choppy bob, and hazelnut eyes framed with lashes a fallow deer would envy, she very thoroughly ticks the box, not for the polished veil of fake perfection as is fashionable, but for the ethereal girl next door.

Amy is the type of woman who can make a cardigan look elegant which would be frumpy and ill fitting on anyone else. But she is also lovely, and has been a trustworthy friend to me since I started at Cranwell Gate.

"Hey Amy, how are you?" I reply, gladdened to see her.

"I'm trying these out" she replies, brandishing a dark blue packet with the words 'Slim Noodles' emblazoned across it.

"Oh hun, you don't need slim noodles, there's nothing of you" I say.

It hasn't escaped my notice that there are still quite a few tubs of Roses, Quality Street, and boxes of other delights left over from Christmas on the table. I open the lid of the Quality Street and reach for my favourite, the toffee penny.

"Well, I admire your iron will, but I need the energy." We both laugh.

"I tell you what, I don't like this new ambre hair look. You know, where the lower two thirds are dyed and not the top?" Amy appears to contemplate this for a moment.

"Well I suppose it saves on hair dye" I offer as I sit at the main table.

Amy tucks her hair behind her ear and regards me seriously. Are you alright Bethan?

I sigh and tell her about Tom and the two conflicting dates in The Blacksmith's Arms I had with him.

"I mean it's not like you have a racist tattoo or something really offensive on show. Just wearing a bit more make up and a necklace?"

"Exactly, and it was a small necklace on my neck, not a long dangling medallion between a heaving cleavage! How can he say it's to get people to look at my breasts? I've never thought of it like that."

"Sounds like you're well rid of him hun."

"It's just such a shame as he was so well mannered and kind before."

"Tell me you've erased his number and blocked him on that dating app."

"Yes I have, and I haven't heard back from him so far, which I'm relieved about"

"Well you can go out with someone else now, forget about that idiot."

"I think I'll have a bit of a break from men now, this all happened in less than a week and its been like a roller-coaster, its exhausting!" I reply, feigning slumping my shoulders.

"Yeah, I bet it really is", Amy says giving my arm a squeeze.

The staff room door opens and Angela Stanton the head teacher beams congenially at me.

"Hi Bethan, I was wondering if you had a minute this afternoon? I thought the school could put together a presentation for the parents and carers about the emotional help we can offer the pupils, and the services we can put people in touch with?"

"Yes, good idea, I'll be free after lunch actually for about half an hour."

"OK, good, yes that's doable, I'll see you then."

Angela Stanton is a good head. Warm hearted and fair, she sees all the children as her own and endeavours to push each one to their potential capabilities. I'll chose to believe that that's only marginally in order to swell the school's Ofsted results.

It's irrational, but she often makes me feel quite nervous. She has to constantly tick so many boxes and please so many people. It can't be easy of course, but I'm never totally sure where her loyalties lie. I'm often reluctant to suggest things because of the budget. Strange sometimes, when you work with a person who, socially would be a great friend, but can make you feel a bit uneasy work wise. Maybe she's a bit unsure of me herself as I don't technically work for the school, but am in the employ of the health authority.

After lunch, I lightly tap on the dark reddish brown door of Angela's office.

"Hi Bethan", Angela says, beaming at me again. "I was thinking of maybe giving a talk to the parents one evening about the emotional help we can offer the pupils, and the support we're able to offer as a school."

I wonder to myself if she always talks to everyone in that Head Teachery type speak.

"Good idea" I nod in agreement, "Shall I draft up some things to say and email them to you today?"

"Well I'll be at the helm so to speak, I'll introduce you and then speak about what we can offer."

I don't mean to sound unkind but Angela's use of jargon really does make me cringe. She means well though.

"OK, sure, shall I list some salient bullet points for you to mention?" I then add "Focussing on what we can offer the students as a school?"

Angela's ears noticeably prick up with the addition of the last question.

"Yes, do that, that'd be great. Thank you Bethan." She beams at me in the way I imagine a great grandparent might beam at a particularly well behaved great grandchild.

Angela fusses around her desk and the adjacent chest of drawers. "I can't seem to find any plain paper" she says.

"Oh not to worry, I've got a couple of new notepads in my bag" I reply.

I undo the toggle on the flap of my leather shoulder bag to retrieve a notebook. My eyes widen in alarm, I push aside the notebooks, pencil case and purse. Marcia Hodge's file which I was working on in the library and I distinctly remember putting in here, has gone.

CHAPTER 9

Patience always pays. Watching people, learning their habits, it's a waiting game.

There you are, leaving the house with your spoilt child. Locking the door with your main set of keys which live in that ugly bag of yours. The spare one in your pocket isn't there is it? You'll put this down to misplacing it somewhere and have to get on as it's already half past eight? Yep, ten out of ten. People are so fucking predictable.

What actually happened was that, whist the annoying little do-gooder was watching some drivel on TV in the lounge, with the door shut so as not to wake Fauntleroy, I opened the letter box.

January nights being dark for so long, it was child's play. Most people are creatures of habit and will always take the path of least resistance. Watching your neighbours for the last week reveals they are no different.

Take one snooker cue with a neodymium pick up magnet attached to the end. Here's one I made earlier. Horrible woollen camel coat hanging on newel post, check. Why these have come back into fashion is beyond me, they were hideous in the nineties, but I digress.

I know you tend to favour the use of the small spare key in the left hand pocket of this monstrosity. Maybe to lend to mummy dearest if the old bat's forgotten hers.

Through the letter box, steady and still. Carefully hover near the left pocket. Down, keep steady....
Bingo.

Pull back gently, slowly, carefully back through again. Two and a half minutes.

The key to the home of the crusader of the wronged. What a complete load of bollocks that act is.

CHAPTER 10

"How are you feeling hun?" I ask a radiantly colossal Fiona.

"Yep, all good, apart from I haven't seen my feet in a while" she smiles. "I was going to pop by yesterday but you had your fancy man round." Her eyes twinkle mischievously.

I laugh, "What?"

"There was a black BMW parked outside your house, I just presumed it was Tom's. How's it going with him? What's his Surname? Let me look him up on Facebook" Fiona says, reaching for her phone.

"Oh no, don't."

Fiona looks concerned so I provide her with an explanation.

"I'm not seeing him any more. I only saw him twice, first time he was absolutely lovely, second time he told me not to wear that necklace Keith bought me as I'm only wearing it to get men to look at my boobs. I'm not planning on making it a hat trick."

"He said what?" Her glowing face is a mask of incredulity.

"Yep, and in a really nasty way. I'm really upset about it quite honestly. And why would he want to sabotage the second date like that? We were getting on so well. Its like he suddenly wanted to upset me."

"I'm lost for words. Bloody hell, there's really nowt so queer as folk is there?"

"Well it's knocked my confidence a bit"

"I bet it has darling, and please don't blame yourself, you weren't to know. Don't think about him for another minute, what a complete weirdo!"

I laugh, I love how down to earth Fiona is. "Coffee from your fancy machine or tea from the kettle?" I ask smiling.

I fill the kettle and turn it on. It's a beautiful Swan one I bought online, with a matching toaster. Turquoise with a sort of diamond pattern. I fill the tea tin with the last of the tea bags from a large PG Tips box and go to put the box in the recycling. Earlier, I wheeled the recycling bin to the front of the house for the bin men to take, which they usually do around noon.

"I'm just taking this out" I inform Fiona. I slip my bare feet into some fluffy unicorn boot slippers which are by the door. I open the door, noting the window sill next to it could do with a dust. It's one of those lovely days you get sometimes in January, where it's nippy but incredibly sunny.

That's funny, the bin's not there. I put it out this morning after I'd walked Dylan to school. Same as I always do on Tuesday mornings. I hope someone else hasn't taken it for themselves. I know the people in the new builds nearby aren't happy about being given those new half sized ones which look suitable for a Sylvanian Family's weekly waste. Have they been creeping around on a bigger bin hunt?

Curiously, I glance the length of the pathway which sits next to the house, on the right. Not there either. I'll call the council and see if they can supply another one, even if it is fun size. I turn to head back into the house, then stop suddenly. There, where I was sure I left it before, is my recycling bin.

Perhaps someone saw me looking around and felt compelled to covertly return it. Maybe it's coincidence, someone took it by mistake and then returned it at that moment. Maybe the bin men have come earlier today and put it back in the wrong place. I lift the lid to put in the PG Tips box.

I scream in shock. On top of all the neatly folded cardboard and old milk bottles, is a dead rat.

It's little eyes are still open, one of it's little arms appears to be reaching out at something. It's long tail is black and wet looking, as though it isn't actually black underneath. It's narrow feet look perfect, petrified in death.

At least there's no blood, rat guts or other innards. I take a deep, steadying breath before re-entering the house. I don't want to worry Fiona. She may have heard my little yelp and already be worried. On opening the door, Fiona calls out "You alright Bee?" The cordial tone in which it is delivered reassures me that she didn't hear anything, just wonders why I took a while.

"Yep, fine. I won't be a minute, just got to do something quickly, then I'll get that kettle on."

I run upstairs to the bathroom. I tear off some loo roll, then on second thoughts decide to take the whole roll. Back outside, I put a couple of squares of the loo roll in my hand and reach for the rat's tail. It looks rather sweet and I feel quite sorry for it. I can't directly feel the tail but the removed sense I can glean through the tissue reminds me of one of those tendrils of spaghetti still left in the colander when you go to wash it up.

The poor creature weighs nothing. I put it on the ground and then on one knee, I set about wrapping it's whole body in loo roll. I try and do this quite tightly as I don't want whoever works in a rubbish sorting out place to get a nasty shock. I know I could bury it, but I don't really know where, so I pick up the soft, white parcel and put it in the refuse bin. I then dart back into the house, run up to the bathroom again and thoroughly wash my hands, resisting the compulsion to pump out every last measure of hand soap.

I smile warmly at Fiona as I come into the kitchen diner, I don't want her to know I was a bit rattled.

"Odd thing happened to me yesterday" I say airily. "I was in the school library, working on a student's file, a girl in year nine I'm working with. I a hundred per cent remember putting the file back into my bag. The head teacher wanted to see me about a presentation she wants to put together on therapy services at the school, so I went to her office, but when I looked in my bag, the file had gone."

Fiona considers this."Yeah that is weird. Did you go anywhere else in between?"

"I went to the staff room to have a lunch I'd bought with me but it was only me and my friend Amy in there the whole time."

"Did you leave the bag for any time?" Fiona asks, intrigued.

"No, I don't think so, frankly I've been driving myself half mad trying to remember."

"Maybe it was in there, you just missed it. Tired, a bit run down, it's easily done."

"Yeah, that's got to be it. It was just scary as it was a student's confidential file. I wouldn't have minded if it'd been something else. Anyway, how are the plans for the nursery coming on?"

Fiona's face lights up with joy. She loves interior design and has relished every aspect of creating a special little room for when Tamsin is born.

"Well, I've got a lady coming next Thursday who's making curtains, a cot bumper, and a cover for a tiny arm chair out of this fabric." Fiona reaches for her bag which I pass to her. She retrieves a small, square swatch of fabric, cut with pinking shears to prevent fraying. It is white with fluffy yellow sheep jumping over gold moons and stars.

"Oh its gorgeous!" I exclaim in that excited tone of voice people reserve especially for babies."What colour are the walls going to be? You couldn't decide last time between that pale green, or the soft yellow."

"It's now going to be pure white, but with accent colours to lift it" replies Fiona animatedly.
Whichever colours she chooses, I know it'll look beautiful, Fiona has exquisite taste and a real eye for design.

I jump as my phone buzzes, still a bit shaken from the surprise in the recycling bin.

"Are you OK Bee?" Fiona asks gently, "You seem on edge. Forget about that idiot, he's not worth worrying about" she leans over and squeezes my knee.

"Like you say, I'm just a bit run down, and I have been a bit upset" I offer in what I hope is a breezy tone.

"Are you going to have a look, see who it is?" Fiona asks.

"No, I'm not one of those people who's on their phone when they're with a friend. I always thinks that's so rude."

"Well I'll let you off this time."

For some reason my guard is up and everything is telling me not to look. To appease Fiona however, I go over to the work top, and retrieve the phone from where I left it by the microwave.

I try not to let it show but relief dilutes every nerve in my body when I see that it's just a message from my network provider informing me how much my bill for the month is, and when it will be due. I smile at Fiona and discreetly breathe a sigh of relief.

Feeling lighter, I go into the kitchen, fill the kettle to half way and flip it on. I'm just about to ask Fiona if she's seen any good box sets lately when my phone chirps again. Because I didn't actually open the last message, just glanced at it, I put this down to it alerting me a second time as I receive two alerts per message. But when I peer at the brightened screen this time to confirm this to myself, I feel the icy fluttering of dread. It's him.

I enter my passcode and reluctantly look at his message. It says; 'How's the slutty school nurse today?'

I walk into the living room, flop down on the sofa next to Fiona and sigh "Tom's sent me a text." I enlighten her of it's contents with a weary sense of resignation. I don't know why exactly, but I sensed I'd receive a less than cordial message from him at some point. I got the impression that, when I saw him last, the viscousness he displayed had not been sated.

"Bastard! He can't do this, it's harassment. Make a note of this and if he sends another one, maybe we could ask the police to have a word with him."

"No I can't do that. The best thing to do with an attention seeker is to not give them attention. It's just embarrassing because it's made me question my judgement of people, which I always thought was good."

"It's no reflection on your judgement. He obviously gets a thrill out of being nasty to people but disguised it well when you first met him."

"He certainly did, he was absolutely lovely then."

"Like Jekyll and Hyde." Fiona adds and I think to myself how an idea in a novel can be pretty disquieting when it's actually happening in your life.

After a while the anchor of Fiona's company makes me feel more relaxed and I try to push thoughts of the rat and the nasty text message to the back of my mind. I need to do quite a large household shop, cleaning products and toiletries as well as freezer and cupboard food, and after school, Dylan's friend is coming over for tea.

Fiona hugs me to her tightly "If you need a friend or if that idiot texts you again, you know where I am" she says kindly. I feel bad as I really didn't want to worry her, but I do feel better for having told her and I know she'd want me to.

I abruptly remember that my friend Andy is coming round today. I consider asking him if we could make it another day as I'm tired, I have work to do, and I've had enough of the soap opera-esque dramas of late. But it might take my mind off things as I always feel relaxed in his company. I decide to drive over to the large Morrisons out of town when I've collected the boys from school.

I move about the house putting everything just so, I can't help myself. Once I've wiped down the draining board, the worktop, the cupboard doors, and aligned the sofa cushions, I feel instantly more calm. I don't know how that rat got into my recycling bin, I don't really want to think about it but perhaps it was down to some bored, wayward kids. Maybe that file was in my bag, I just missed it. Except that I know it wasn't.

Andy comes round after lunch. He gives me a large bar of Galaxy chocolate as he comes in.

"Your favourite" he smiles, wrapping his long arms around me.

Andy is tall with mid blue eyes and hair the colour of vivid burnt umber. He is one of those long limbed men who are quite rangy and would have to put on a lot of weight in order to be anything close to fat. He always smells like a forest newly cleansed in rain, and his rich, deep voice is pure South London.

I'm not sure which particular bit of London Andy grew up in as he doesn't much talk about it. I get the impression that that part of his life hurts him and is neatly packed away in a box in the attic of his mind. If hurt can ever be neat.

Andy told me that he moved here two years ago as he discovered he had a sister, Caroline of who's existence he had never known and who was terminally ill. He moved here to be near her, get to know and offer comfort to her in her final months. When Caroline passed away, Andy decided to stay in the area having found a home and job he loved.

He didn't really know anyone, so he joined the historical society of which I'm a member. People in the area who love reading about history, like me, meet up usually around once a month. Alan Palmer who runs the group emails us all and we gather in the community hall to indulge ourselves in conversations which non-historical fans would consider to be a very effective cure for insomnia. I went over to the tall, red headed man who'd appeared by the tea table one day, nervously nibbling a chocolate digestive. We immediately got talking about Medieval Armenia, and the animated way his eyes lit up, I knew I'd found a friend.

That was around six months ago and we've fallen into a contented friendship ever since. I like him, I feel I can really trust him and I love his quirky taste, he often sends me links to offbeat places, books or people of the past.

"How have you been Bethan?" Andy asks me, and I tell him about work, and Tom and his capricious mood swings. I feel better for getting it off my chest as I knew I would.

"What a muppet, do you want me to have a word?" Andy offers and I smile deeply from my soul for the first time in a week, feeling safe and OK again.

Andy and I settle into one of our quirky conversations, the trajectory of which can range from bog bodies preserved perfectly from the middle ages to Victorian worker's rights, or lack of them. I allow myself to enjoy the refreshing sense of being taken to another place, as becoming immersed in a good conversation with a friend can.

"Have a look at this" Andy says holding out his phone on which a photo show's a corpulent black and white cat wearing an expression which suggests it isn't happy about being disturbed from a nap. It is also wearing a red and white Father Christmas hat adorned with a holly sprig and topped with a small gold bell.

"That's Sam, my new cat. She's a rescue. She's gorgeous. I love how animals just love you unconditionally, not like humans."

I see a flicker of sadness pass Andy's eyes. I smile and nod my agreement, it is true. "I was thinking of maybe getting a rabbit or hamster for Dylan" I muse, "From that new pet shop which has opened on the high street. I wonder where I could put a hutch, maybe in the utility room?"

"What the hell?" I mutter to myself. The photo of Mum and I outside the Belvedere in Vienna lives in a mirrored glass frame on the side table by the sofa. Why then is it encased in the saffron coloured Indian frame on the shelf with the little mirrors embroidered on which contains the picture of Dylan on his 1st birthday? Or usually does. I'm going to get an early night tonight, I'm more tired than I thought.

CHAPTER 11

The world is full of people like you. Most of them run it, elitist, privileged, entitled lovies.

You've just been able to move on as if nothing happened. That bloody place hasn't tarnished your soul at all, or made you loose your ability to believe in anything.

Right, that pathetic old lush over the road will be having a nap now. Perfect. In we go. Can't do anything too obvious, like swapping your shampoo for drain cleaner or something, much as I'd like to. No, this visit will be a restrained art form. Conjure fright and questioning, rather than anger.

The sense of your happy family is everywhere. Smug pictures of the two of you. Lets have a move about shall we, make the caped crusader think she's going senile. Put that one of le dauphin in there, that's it, and one of you and Mumsy in this gaudy creation.

Oh look, one of those pretentious coffee machines. Cappuccino, espresso, latte, latte macchiato just by pressing one button. When did people stop drinking normal coffee? When the privileged lovies who rule the world started designing shit like this. Is there a box of those stupid little pods one needs to insert into this nearby? Ah there is, in the adjacent food cupboard. I'll take those. What will the avenging angel do without a latte macchiato? Whatever that is.

Just a couple more touches, a picture frame or two turned round, a couple of books and ubiquitous, trashy ornaments swapping places. Make you look twice and wonder. Oh, maybe I could leave messages with flowers, floriography. I wonder which one means evil bitch?

The happy family bathroom. Oh Ted Baker bubble bath, the more ple-beian end of the designer sweep, but it makes you feel special doesn't it. All gone, rinsed down the drain, bottle filled with water and re-placed. Didn't have any sulphuric acid today.

Just lighting these candles. Your house is so ordered, I know you'll no-tice. Maybe you do have demons after all? Only yours are controlled aren't they? Not eating into you like maggots in cheese every waking moment. Just a few more touches. I can always return. Tempting to leave the key on the table just to see your face, but no. Surreptitious is the order of the day. A marathon and not a sprint. I'll slip this key back into the pocket of that repugnant coat at the first opportunity. I'll use the one I had cut to return at my leisure.

CHAPTER 12

The car doors slam as Dylan and his friend Oliver drag out their rucksacks and dash towards the house. I follow in their wake with the shopping I've bought from the large Morrisons. "Shoes off boys" I say as I unlock the door. Two pairs of soft, black Velcro shoes are hastily deposited in the hallway before their respective owners shoot up the stairs to Dylan's room.

As I move about the kitchen putting things away, I turn on the radio to take my mind off recent events. I smile as a song I love from the nineties fills the room. Whilst turning on the grill and collecting together the things for the freezer, I feel an irrational yet very real, eerie sense of being watched. I suppose I'm feeling a bit sensitive from earlier.

I fill a saucepan with water and place it on the hob to boil. I then take the loo roll, toothpaste and soaps I have bought and cross the kitchen diner to take them upstairs. I smile as I see Dylan and Oliver in the lounge larking about. I stop dead, the photo from Vienna with my Mum is now back inside the mirrored glass frame, and the photo of Dylan on his first birthday, the Indian one. Maybe I imagined them ever being otherwise.

I put the products into their respective homes in the bathroom. The scented tea lights on the window sill have blackened wicks and deep ravines in the wax. But I hadn't lit them. Or had I? Perhaps I had and am muddled up. I feel my memory is turning into a quicksand of unreliability where everything is surreal and nothing can be relied upon.

In the kitchen I peel some potatoes and try to escape into the

Brit pop songs I know every word to. I sheathe my feet into my slippers and go out into the garden to pick some rosemary from the stone trough of herbs I have out there. I can't seem to shake the feeling of being watched. How do you know if it's a sixth sense or just paranoia? Of course its paranoia I chide myself and pick several sprigs from the soft needled plant.

Suddenly I hear a loud bang like something heavy being dropped. It sounds as though it came from the pathway behind the garden. Tentatively, I cross the lawn over to the fence and look out onto the pathway. I realise I've subconsciously been hugging my jumpered arms around myself.

There is nobody there and the air doesn't have that sense of having been disturbed. I take a deep breath. And then I see it. Vile pornographic images from a magazine have been stapled to the back of my fence. Not glamorous, oiled bodies feigning ecstasy, but disgusting, deviant forms of heterosexual intercourse stare back at me. Some of the edges gently flap in the breeze lending a cruel touch of reality to a nightmare. There must be thirty pages here, in colour, in each one the woman looking cowed. Oh God, it's truly awful.

One picture shows a lady with brown hair in a half up messy ponytail. She's wearing a white lacy basque and white stockings, but has what looks like weights hanging from her private parts, an expression of discomfort contorting her features. In another, a man appears to be entering a lady from behind, his hands pulling back the corners of her mouth, apparently for more purchase. Her eyes are wide and fearful. I want to be sick.

The pictures look professional and I suppose the women are actresses, mercifully it can't be real.

"Right OK" I say to myself, taking a breath. I unlock the gate and take down every single decrepit image, the thought of people finding these erotic sickening me further.

As with the incident in the pub, I surprise myself by how calm I am. I never before realised I had such a calm resolve I could call on under pressure. I swiftly and methodically remove each gruesome image from the fence. I don't even want the staples there either. One of them is loose and sits proud of the wooden panel into which it has been interred so I ply it out with my fingers. I then use this one as a tool with which to gouge the other staples out of my fence.

I don't know how much time has gone past, but what I guess to be around fifteen minutes later, I have every despicable image folded together and a pile of silver staples in a neat, defeated looking pile on the ground. I stand up, feeling a little dizzy, my back aching in protest. It doesn't matter, I need to get rid of this stuff, that's all that does.

I look around me to see if there are any other errant pieces of the pictures. There don't appear to be. The pathway is clear and still. I walk quickly into the house and throw the lot into my kitchen bin. I then remove the liner, I don't want this filth polluting my home so I tie the liner up. Shaking and almost crying, I take a roll of new liners from the cleaning cupboard and put the whole thing into another one. Then another. I furiously tie several knots in the lot as if to contain forever its dark contents.

I put the liner into the refuse bin and go back into the house. Dylan's friend Oliver is upstairs and I need to keep a cool head and get through this evening. I realise I completely forgot to put fish fingers under the grill for the three of us. I retrieve some sausages from the fridge, they won't take as long. I put some peas on to boil and drain the pan of potatoes. These simple tasks calm me. I mix some butter into the potatoes and mash them. I'm not adding rosemary, I don't want to go out there again. A little salt, no pepper, Dylan's not a fan.

Who the hell would do that? Was it Tom? Was it kids? On the day I found that dead rat? I don't think so. How can I ever protect children and young people if this is lurking in the bowels of the world? It'll be a while before I stop seeing that sordid stuff, whatever the hell it was when I close my eyes.

I inhale what I hope is a steadying breath into my frazzled body.

"Boo!" says a voice behind me poking me lightly in my lower back.

I scream in pure, primal fear, the pan of potatoes clattering onto the floor. The worry, confusion and fright I've been feeling rushing from me like a burst dam.

A crestfallen Dylan and an unsure Oliver look back wide eyed at me.

"I'm sorry Mum we were just playing detectives" Dylan offers in a small voice. "I'm Holmes and Oliver's Watson."

I put my hand over my mouth, stifling a sob."I'm so, so sorry darlings" I say, reaching out to hug both of them. Both little bodies hesitantly hug me back though their wariness cuts me. "Mummy's just had a really bad day. Let's order a pizza shall we."

CHAPTER 13

I shouldn't have done that, actual criminal damage, that was sloppy. Could lead back to me before I'm ready, before I've had some more recreation. Truth is, those kids I paid to do it reminded me of myself. Already tossed on the pile of life's surplus. The dregs. Just needing to feel needed, excited, if only for a short while. At least they've got each other and one of them hasn't been left alone in the world.

CHAPTER 14

The last two days seem to have gone by without incident. No weird object displacement or gruesome finds.

I'm so angry. How dare Tom think he think he can paper my fence like that. What have I actually done to him where he feels he has the right to do such a thing? Did he think that the comment about my wearing the necklace was perfectly reasonable and is angry because I walked out? Even if he did, would that really warrant this sort of action? And when he knew I'd see it. Was he watching me? I seldom use that path and I wouldn't have known that stuff was there for ages if I hadn't been in the garden at that moment.

Of course I wish I'd taken pictures now, gone to the police with tangible proof of some sort of viscous smear campaign. I wish he'd never walked me home that time, I had no idea I was going to be in for all this. He knows I have a child in the house with me.

Although nothing seems to have happened in the last couple of days, I can't really relax. I don't feel as though a storm is over, but that another one may be brewing. My nerves have been constantly on alert since, like soldiers awaiting a signal to attack the enemy.

I couldn't sleep at all the night it happened, though last night I slept deeply as I was so very tired. I remember it making me feel kind of wanted, like a prize when I first saw how proprietorial Tom could be. How intent he was on making sure the dates were still happening. But that rapidly slipped into the realm of uneasiness which has then, more recently blossomed into full on consternation. How can someone accelerate from being a bit too pushy to this level of maliciousness in less than a fortnight?

Right, I'm going to be smarter. Catalogue any events and take pictures of any subsequent damage to my property which I can then approach the police with. He's covering his tracks because he hasn't actually sent me anything threatening. Plus I've no actual proof that Tom did any of this. Somehow I know for certain that he did though.

Dylan, Oliver and I had a nice evening after the incident with the fence. I was determined not to worry the boys and in no time they were once more their cheerful selves.

***

The room in the school in which I see any student who wishes to talk confidentially to me is small and quite dark.

"Why do you think that is?" I gently ask Tim Cohen who wants, with all his being to become a girl known as Sophia.

I see several children like Tim. Boys who dearly want to be girls, girls who wish they were boys, and both sexes who wish to be classed as non-gender specific. I do my best to offer kindness and guidance. While there are those who will carry the feeling of being born inside the wrong body into later life until they can obtain a physical change, most are confused and just need someone to listen to them.

The bell signifying lunch time trills. Tim collects up his bag and smiles widely at me. He doesn't seem at all dejected about life in general, and I often see him holding court with ease among large groups of pupils, boys and girls. I too collect my things together. I've been extra careful about doing this since the incident in the library. Though I don't want it to turn into a debilitating obsessive, compulsive ritual. They won't govern me any more.

I eat lunch in the canteen today. I buy a coronation chicken sandwich which I accompany with some smokey bacon flavoured crisps. Sod the diet, I need the energy. I discreetly look inside my bag to check my phone. We're not really allowed phones in school, though they don't mind them used with discretion. Still no text from Tom, good. I wonder if I should also check my emails, perhaps he's been able to apprehend my email address by some means.

I notice that I have received a text from Andy which, unusually for him is very brief and to the point.

'Hi Bethan, hope you're well. Just wondered if I could pop round quickly later? xx'

Andy's never sent such a text before, we've arranged to meet up sure but usually in amongst a deep or quirky conversation about history, or places he'd like to visit.

I type back: 'Hi Andy, yeah sure, I'll be home around five. Are you OK? xx'

School passes easily and I feel the heightened sense of fear diminishing. Maybe feeling relaxed and safe again is a possibility now. I picked up a few things from the Sainsbury's local on the way home. Some salmon fish cakes, a mixed salad, some of those biscuits Dylan likes; Pick Ups, and some flowers for my mum.

I enter the house to the sound of heartfelt laughter which makes me smile. It's glorious contagiousness compels me to go straight up to the living room to investigate. Mum and Dylan sit watching *Horrible Histories* together.

"Hi!" I say brightly, kissing both Mum and Dylan on the cheek and giving Mum the posy of roses, daisies and gypsophila I bought.

"Oh they're lovely darling, how was your day?"

SNIPS AND SNAILS

"Pretty good thanks" I reply, genuinely feeling this, "Yours?"

"Oh yes, we've just been watching this, it's very funny"

The 'Stupid Deaths' segment appears, prompting fresh laughter from it's captive audience, so I smile, squeeze Mum's shoulder, and head downstairs.

I take off my coat and shoes. I feel a bit bad as I'm always telling Dylan not to wear his shoes around the house, but being among the warmth and laughter of my mum and son was so welcome and I'm glad I didn't miss a moment of it in which to remove mine. It reminded me that this is my real life, filled with warmth and safety. Not some maniacal vendetta from a guy I went on a couple of dates with.

Whilst putting away the bits of shopping I bought, I notice a text from Andy.

'OK. I'll swing by around half past xx' it says.

That'll be any minute now. I'm keen to know what's on his mind. My Mum comes down into the kitchen and swathes her small body in her duvet like dusky pink coat. "

"I'll let you two have your dinner in peace then." Mum beams at me.

"OK, Thanks for picking him up. See you tomorrow yeah?" I'm so grateful to my Mum for collecting Dylan from school for me to facilitate my job at Cranwell Gate.

"Bye Grandma" says Dylan hugging mum tightly by the door as she's encasing her feet into some small, furry UGG style boots.

"Bye love" she answers, kissing Dylan on the head.

Dylan comes over to me in the kitchen area and I hug him. "What did you do at school today sweetheart?" I ask him.

He thinks intently as though it occurred a year ago and then replies excitedly "learnt about Barcelona. Can we go there one day Mum? You, me and Grandma?"

"Yeah definitely darling, lets do it" I smile.

There is a quick, sharp knock at the door, that'll be Andy. As I let him in, I realise he's never actually met Dylan before. I once read that you should always introduce the youngest person to the eldest first. Though that was probably when knights rescued damsels from towers and people you'd been on dates with didn't start campaigns against you.

"Hiya, are you alright?" I ask Andy. His forget -me -not blue eyes register a look of worry.

"Sweetheart, this is my good friend Andy, Andy this is my son Dylan" I inform each proudly.

"Hi Dylan" Andy says and I'm pleased he doesn't offer it in too forceful a tone like some adults do with children.

"Hi" Dylan replies politely but somewhat shyly.

"Come through, I'll make us a coffee" I say, noticing that Dylan has slipped back upstairs again.

"Everything alright?" I ask Andy, he looks quite pale and obviously wants to talk immediately, so I usher him over to the table where we each pull out a chair and sit down.

"Not really" Andy sighs. "This came through my door today and I thought it might have been from that rogue you were seeing. Andy dips into his pocket and timidly brings out a folded piece of white a4 paper which he passes to me.

"What's this?" I say, apprehensively taking the paper and opening it up. The two lines I reveal make my breath catch and I feel a flutter of nervous adrenalin seep into my chest.

'To the ginger cunt who's banging Bethan,
be careful, she's had more pricks than a second hand dart board.'

My teeth clench together, I'm livid. How dare he presume to send such disgusting letters to my friends.

I sigh, "Right well we can take this to the police and they can dust it for finger prints. I'm absolutely furious, he's not going to get away with this. Just imagine if I'd actually done something to upset him. I'm so sorry Andy."

"We can't prove it was him though."

"Doesn't matter, let's go to the station in the high street right now, make a report."

Andy seems calmer, more measured. "I don't think they could do anything though hun" he offers, shrugging.

"Yes they could, they could have a word with him."

"Then he'd likely be more angry."

"No, bullies are cowards at heart, if you stand up to them they slither off."

"OK, well it's your call. I was worried about telling you but I have now." Andy's relief at having told me is unmistakable, and I feel so sorry for him being worried all day.

"I'm really sorry he sent you that" I say, contrition narrowing my eyes.

"Don't bother me if he hasn't got anything better to do. Bothers me if he upsets you though. Muggy little Prick."

Something about the way Andy says this so matter of factly causes me to burst out laughing. I don't know why, I am upset but Andy's resigned, lopsided grin and shrug of his gangling shoulders comforts me and makes me feel OK again.

I theatrically draw in a nourishing breath as if to signify starting anew. "Right, I'm not going to let that idiot ruin my evening, Dylan and I are going out. I need a change of scene and take my mind of things."

"Oh, OK, where are you going?" Andy asks looking entirely perplexed. I can see how it would look to a good friend, I'm usually more measured in my actions and decisions, and have probably come across as quite manic and erratic in this one. But I need to summon all my strength together to get through this, stay strong for Dylan, and stop myself going insane with worry. Plus a change of scene seems blissful.

Andy has always been very reluctant to meet in cafes, restaurants and the like whenever I've suggested it before. At his behest, he has always come to my house when we've spent time together, outside of the historical club. He says he gets anxious, is unable to relax and feels that people are looking at and judging him. This being so, I realise it may seem insensitive to ask him but I don't want him to think I'm not including him if I don't and God knows, I need to get out or I'll go stir crazy. I've always loved this house, but lately I just haven't felt safe here. I'm angry with myself, why did I ever allow a stranger to know my address?

I run upstairs to Dylan's room, squeezing Andy's arm affectionately as I pass. I knock lightly on Dylan's door and gently push it open.

"Hi Mum" Dylan says without taking his eyes off his tablet.

"Hi sweetheart, I wondered if you fancied going out for dinner tonight? I'm a bit too tired to cook. We can go anywhere you like darling."

I now have Dylan's undivided attention.

"Pizza Express?" he asks, wide eyed with hope.

"Yep" I nod. "Get your coat and shoes on."

I feel better now I'm putting this into motion. I go back downstairs into the kitchen where Andy is still seated at the dining table. A look on his face suggests he doesn't know what to make of my bizarre reaction.

"I'm not going to let him get me down" I tell Andy, seeking to reassure him, I can tell he's worried about me.

"Dylan and I are going to Pizza Express. I know it's not really your cup of tea, but if you'd like to join us you'd be more than welcome, my treat."

Andy's eyes soften."Yeah OK, that'd be lovely" he replies.

Pizza Express is set in a lovely Georgian building with a grand facade, only slightly faded with the passage of time. As we wait to be seated, it warms me that people dining would probably assume Andy, Dylan and I were a family. Mum, Dad, and son out on a chilly evening for a feast of carbohydrates. I realise I like this feeling and stand a little taller.

"Hi, table for three?" asks a very slim young man with one of those fashionable hipster beards and almost every facial orifice pierced.

"Yes please" I smile back excitedly. I really need to get out more.

It saddens me slightly that Dylan no longer wants to grab the tiny pale of stubby wax crayons and giddily fill in the word search on the kid's menu. He's at that age now where he's no longer a young kid, but not quite a big one. I incline my head toward the young man as he seats us at a small, square table and discreetly ask in a quiet voice if I could also have a kids menu in the manner one might use to score drugs.

"Hi Bethan!" exclaims an excited female voice. I turn to see Fiona and John waving us over from one of those trendy long, shared tables toward the back of the room.

"Hey, there's my friends Fiona and John, shall we go and say hello?" I ask Andy tentatively. He doesn't strike me as one for great gatherings and sure enough, I see a faint trace of dismay pass across his features. His natural good grace prevails how-ever, and he nods with a warm smile.

"Hi guys, this is my friend Andy" I say in order to make Andy feel included from the outset."These are my friends Fiona and John."

I quickly go over to Fiona who is attempting to rise to hug me.

"Hi Dylan, how are you?" Fiona asks Dylan, her skin glowing like buffed gold in the twinkling tea light flames.

"Good thanks" replies Dylan. He loves Fiona and John.

I furtively engineer what I think will be the most judicious seating arrangement. Andy and I opposite Fiona and John, with Dylan sitting on the end, between myself and Fiona. As I ask John about his work, and tell Andy of it, with Fiona asking Dylan about what he's been learning at school, I feel a slight awkward-ness. I don't think too much about it though, that's just what happens when you have separate friends with different inter-ests. John gets on with everyone and would never concede of such tension. I read once that when an adult is unsure of how to act, they resort to coping as they did when they were a small child. I do feel very slightly like a shiny toy with which both Andy and Fiona want to play.

A waitress comes over, pen and pad poised to take our orders. I order a Diet Coke and the chicken pasta for me, and for Dylan, (who it turns out, was happy to chose from the kid's menu) asks for the dough balls, an apple juice and the cheese and tomato pasta. He also asks for the chocolate ice cream sundae which the waitress says will come later.

Dylan shrugs "I just love ice cream."

"Who doesn't?" replies John.

 The waitress turns to Andy to take his order and her eyes widen in apparent recognition "Oh hello Sean, blimey it's been a while, I thought you'd moved away."

Andy looks up at her, nonplussed. "I'm sorry love, I don't know who you mean."

She puts her hand to her chest, imploring him to recognise her "Kelly Peters" she offers.

It is painfully apparent that everyone at the table is feeling awkward and embarrassed. Both for Andy, who has no idea who this lady is mistaking him for, and for Kelly who clearly believes otherwise.

Fiona quickly interjects,"I thought I saw a friend of mine the other day who has black curly hair, like Cher. I saw what I thought was her hair and I was like "hiya!! "and she turned round and it wasn't her! I was mortified." Kelly noticeably relaxes a little and I smile at Fiona.

John adds, "Someone I went to school with didn't recognise me on Facebook! I added them and they said, "do I know you?" I was so embarrassed!"

Kelly regains her composure gracefully and carries on with the order, though her eyes betray a look of complete disbelief.

"That was weird." I say comradely to Andy when Kelly has gone.

As the meal progresses, Dylan and Andy seem to be getting on really well. I really appreciate Andy coming here with me, I know he doesn't particularly enjoy this sort of thing.

Fiona asks me how my day was and I resist the urge to tell her about the letter.

"Hey, why don't you give that other fellow a try" she suggests enthusiastically.

"Give him a try?" I say laughing.

"Go on a date with him. The other one, I preferred him anyway."

"I think Tom did quite an effective job of never making me want to date anyone ever again" I say cynically.

"Oh don't let the bastard grind you down!" replies Fiona, speedily putting both hands over her mouth like the speak no evil monkey when she realises Dylan has heard her choice of noun.

"Don't worry Fiona, I've heard loads of naughty words." Dylan declares matter-of-factly. I good naturedly roll my eyes and we all giggle.

As we all gather together our belongings to leave the restaurant, I spontaneously hug Andy. "Thanks so much for looking out for me" I tell him. Even through his jumper I can feel the sharp contours of his bones against my cheek. And something else too, his heart thudding.

CHAPTER 15

I rise early the next morning refreshed and renewed. I usually get up at around half past seven, but had made my bed and was about before six today which lent me some semblance of control and empowerment. Although I feel a little tense, I'm just so delighted with the way I dealt with things yesterday. Victoriously, and not allowing a bully to topple me over. Bethan one, Tom nil.

The memory of that letter and it's vile, misogynistic language feels rather like an angry, yet healed scar now. A visceral reminder of an incident you've survived long ago. The thought of it angers me yet it doesn't posses any power over me now. It has lost it's might, it's potency, no longer do I feel a sensation of dread and fear snaking up my spine.

It's too early to text Fiona or rouse Dylan, so I busy myself by making a coffee and looking at some student's files. Later on I'll go through Dylan's clothes and the ones which are now too small for him, I'll take to the Salvation Army clothing bank.

***

It's glorious weather today and I'm so pleased to be finishing at two thirty and then spending the afternoon with Fiona. We could sit in the garden, or maybe go into town and buy some things for baby Tamsin.

I pull up outside Fiona's large, white, detached residence. It's marvellously uplifting to hear the birds singing, summoning the onset of an early spring. The sun is low in the sky, and I feel a sense of rejuvenation washing over me. As though I can now shed the skin of worry and fear, whatever nasty pranks or messages he sends my way, Tom has succeeded only in making me feel stronger.

A tired, deflated looking Fiona tentatively answers the door.

"Bethan? Oh shit, sorry I forgot you were coming over". Her eyes look red and puffy as though she has recently been crying.

I can honestly say I've never seen Fiona anything less than charismatic and sparkling, like a shaken up can of fizzy drink. This subdued demeanour perturbs me.

"Oh that's OK, no worries at all, I can always come another time if you like?"

"No it's alright, come in." She opens the door and attempts a smile but looks completely drained, more than that, hurt, dejected.

"Are you alright?" I ask cautiously.

"Yeah, I'm fine hun" she smiles, in a kind of half warm, half sad way. "I've just been being so sick, I puked more than twenty times yesterday, at twenty four I lost count."

"What? That's awful."

"Yeah, we went to hospital and they wanted me to do a urine test, then I was sick in the waiting room. It was a lot of pointless waiting around to be honest, them telling me to drink lemonade, eat digestive biscuits and wear those sea sickness bands."

"Oh no" I say. I feel a bit gormless but I don't know what to suggest. I wasn't sick once when I was pregnant with Dylan and I wish my hair and skin still looked as good as they did then.

"Is there anything I can do?" I want to be of practical help. "I could go to the shops for you mate, if you fancy anything."

"Well I was eating a digestive pissing biscuit earlier, and was then actually being sick while I was trying to eat it. How about that."

"Oh no, how awful. Let me get the kettle on, you go and sit down."

Fiona smiles and makes her way slowly into the living room.

I go into the sumptuous kitchen. The sun is streaming in through the double hung widows, bathing everything in shimmering, flaxen light.

I fill the kettle and put it on to boil. The familiar trill, which only days ago I came to dread signals the arrival of a text. I enjoy the feeling of removal from this now. Whatever it says, its not going to break, or even hurt me. Sure enough, it's him. A mere sigh indicates my displeasure, I'm still in one piece, breathing normally. I smile, he's lost. I calmly view the message;

'Do you still think about me? xx'

Hasn't he got anything better to do than seek to remind me of his pitiful existence? It's beyond pathetic. I resolve to go back onto the dating site and meet another guy. Put this sorry scenario firmly to bed.

I suddenly realise, I didn't ask Fiona which drink she wanted, she often favours hot chocolate over tea and coffee. I go back through to the living room. As I approach, I can see Fiona on the sofa. She's looking at her phone, the trace of an impish smile playing on her lips. I'm glad she's looking better, I was genuinely worried. As I enter the living room, her eyes stretch in something close to horror. And something else, guilt, and I watch, confused as my best friend hastily attempts to construct a scene where she wasn't taking forbidden rapture in looking at something on her phone.

CHAPTER 16

"What's going on?" I ask slowly.

"What? Nothing" Fiona replies, trying to hard to convince herself.

"I'm going to go" I say quietly, feeling tears stinging the backs of my eyes. Could it have been Fiona who sent me that text? Even though it came up with Tom's name, and I've spoken to Tom on this number? Has she been behind the pranks? Or helping him carry them out? Why?

"Bethan, wait" Fiona utters, so quietly I can barely hear.

I try to walk sedately back into the room, my feet feel like lead.

Fiona sighs. She seems to collect her thoughts for a beat, then speaks guardedly. She has a cream waffle throw around herself but seems to shiver slightly. She twists the tassels on the edge. I am vaguely aware of the kettle boiling in the kitchen.

"You know when I was helping in my sister's gift shop about a year ago?" she asks softly.

"Yeah" I reply in a timid voice.

"Well," she looks pained, as though the act of speaking is difficult, "There was this guy who used to come in a lot. Brian."

"OK" I say, warily.

"We got to know each other, became friends, and he'd come in to see me pretty much every day." She looks at me and then quickly away again. "We fell in love."

I'm incredulous, I cant imagine Fiona ever with anyone but John.

"He knew I was married," she continues, "but he just made me laugh, feel alive, feel attractive."

"But doesn't John make you feel those things?" I truly can't believe I'm hearing this, Fiona and John have always seemed like the ideal couple, they come alive in one another's company.

"He does, he's lovely, and that's why I feel so awful."

"OK" I say again, trying to sound neutral.

"I know it sounds cliched, but I just felt so alive and vital with Brian. I know John's an absolute sweetheart, and I do love him, but we've been together since I was seventeen and it's just become so pedestrian. I've never craved anyone else, or cheated on John, but when I met Brian, it made me realise, I've never really done anything. I've never been on a girlie holiday, I've never tried drugs, I've never even been to a nightclub."

I listen intently, I had no idea Fiona harboured such feelings.

"It's not that I don't love John, or like him as a person, I do. And I am happy with him and I know how lucky I am to have such a good man."

"You can't help how you feel, please don't feel guilty on my account" I implore her, genuinely feeling bad for her now I realise the depths of the discomfort she's been feeling.

"I just always looked forward to seeing Brian in a way I never have with John." Fiona meets my gaze and shrugs, a look of helplessness gnarling her lovely face.

"Anyway, he's got back in touch recently through Facebook and it's reminded me of him. He says he misses me and still has feelings for me."

67

"Is?" I nod very surreptitiously in the direction of Fiona's colossal stomach.

"No, no I never slept with Brian. Just kissed him. He doesn't even know I'm pregnant, unless he's seen a picture of me on Facebook maybe."

Fiona appears deep in thought for a few seconds, then says, "It just shocked me, he sent me a Facebook message last night and I was feeling so sick and I've not had any time to really process it all. I'm happy with John, I'm glad we're starting a family, I just dearly wish I'd lived a bit more."

The words tumble out of Fiona as she stifles sobs." For nearly twenty years we've just been working our arses off to build our dream of having a family and being happy and I just don't know if my heart's in it any more, but its a bit bloody late isn't it."

I let out a deep sigh, I don't know what to think. Awful and selfish as it sounds though, I'm relieved that Fiona hasn't had anything to do with the pranks, though I feel a wailing sadness for her.

"I had no absolutely no idea" I say honestly.

"No one has, not even my sister. I knew when you marry there may be people to come into your life who take your fancy and I hoped the feelings for Brian would subside, which they did" Fiona looks reflective.

"But now he's got back in touch it's brought it all up again?" I offer.

"Exactly" she nods.

"But I'm sure there are pictures of you on there where you're clearly pregnant, and it says you're married. Though obviously he knew that anyway. What if he knows you're pregnant and has sent the message because he's jealous or something."

Fiona's chin disappears into her neck "That's a bit dark isn't it?"

I raise my eyebrows in resignation, "People can surprise you" I say.

I make Fiona a hot chocolate and she begins to look a bit brighter.

"You could peruse things with this Brian but if he doesn't know you're pregnant, how would he feel? Or you could have the baby, then get in touch with him, it's not long now." I feel so disloyal to John who has never been anything other than kindness itself to me. But you only get one life and if Fiona is this unhappy, I don't want to make her feel any worse about how John's world would crumble if she did leave him, which it would.

"Or you could erase Brian on Facebook and concentrate on John. If you'd been married to Brian for nearly twenty years and then met John in a setting where you're seeing him at his best, he'd feel exciting as well wouldn't he? It's just human nature to crave something you think might be better."

I shrug trying to be as rational as possible, "If you're really not happy with John, you don't have to be with him. But what if you left John and then were not happy with Brian either? Could the two of you get some counselling perhaps?"

Fiona lets out a long breath. "Maybe" she says, staring into the middle distance. "Anyway, how's everything with you?"

"Oh absolutely fine hun, don't worry about me."

"Oh please talk to me about something else, I'm driving myself up the wall. Did Tom text again?"

"He did, just a minute ago actually, but I'm past caring about him."

"Good" says Fiona, and it warms my heart to see her smile.

"Are you going to go out with that other guy? Pete wasn't it?"

"No, I shouldn't think he's on there any more. I'm going to go back on though and see if I can match with someone who isn't a complete psychopath." I smile widely for comic effect and am rewarded with a tinkling peel of laughter from Fiona.

"Someone to take your mind off that doughnut" she offers.

"That's a bit unfair" I reply, "I love doughnuts." We relax into the welcome tonic of easy laughter, both of us feeling better.

***

Poor Fiona, I wonder what she's going to do. It can't be an easy decision either way. I mull this over as I cut pithy, loving quotes from some coloured paper I printed off at school. I've bought one of those multi photo frames as a present for Fiona when baby Tamsin arrives. Soft pastel pink, green, peach, lilac and baby blue wooden heart frames intertwined. I thought I'd insert a little lovable quote into each; 'The littlest feet make the biggest footprints in our hearts', 'From small beginnings come great things' etc. I got the idea from a cafe nearby which has quotes from famous people inserted into frames. It saddens me that it's probably unwise now to use 'Your first breath took ours away' just in case Fiona and John do split up and the gift lives in one of Tamsin's bedrooms with one parent, a lonesome echo of a lost trinity.

I think about what Fiona said. I hate the thought of either of them being unhappy, John because Fiona leaves him or Fiona because she does not. I think too of Fiona mentioning that guy Pete, and I feel myself smile. It's been nearly three weeks now since we said "Hi" on the dating site. I put down the piece of paper I'm cutting to fit one of the heart frames and pull up the app on my phone. I haven't been on it in a while and it asks me to log in again. I know its stupid but I have the same passwords for everything – DylanA1234.

I see the pictures of me I chose, which I thought were the most flattering, and the write up underneath which I dearly hope isn't too cheesy. I look under 'messages' and see the photo of Tom which so captivated me only a short time ago. I feel nothing as I calmly delete him. It presents me with a list of possible reasons for this decision, though 'because they are completely unbalanced' doesn't appear to be an option and so I select 'No Reason'.

I see Pete's photo is still there and so this means he still has the app and therefore is presumably still single. I type out 'Hey x' to him and feel a tremor of excitement as I press 'send'.

I put the radio on before sitting back at the table to resume my cutting. Within ten minutes I receive a response, 'Hey yourself xx' it says.

CHAPTER 17

The last of the winter has gone, it's a wonderfully sunny February. It's Saturday morning and I'm sorting out Dylan's clothes as some have seemingly rapidly become too small for him. I don't really know anyone at the school with younger boys to offer them to, so they'll go to charity.

I've told Dylan that I'll take him and a friend out today. Maybe to the cinema in town or for a burger. Or maybe we could chuck their bikes in the car and drive along to the coast, so they can ride them along the promenade. I always find the arrival of the sun so sanative, perhaps I'll become a pagan and worship it.

I see the dating app on my phone has a small number one beside it, signifying a message. I smile to myself, I hope its from Pete. I'm pleased to see that it is, around half an hour ago he sent:

'Hey Bethan, how's your weekend going? Xxx'

I type back 'Hi, good th...'

"Mum, where are we going today? Can Oliver come?" Dylan's zeal bisects my wool-gathering like a sword through an apple.

"Hi sweetheart, one minute, I'm just sending a message."

"Are you texting Emma?"

"One minute Dylan OK, and then I will."

I quickly type back 'Hi, good thanks, yourself?' then instantly wish I'd included more detail. That probably seemed completely uninspiring. I pull myself together and remind my mouth muscles to shift upwards.

"OK darling, Oliver and not another friend instead?" I love Oliver, he and Dylan have a great friendship. I worry though that if Oliver is ever off sick or if they fall out, Dylan may not have any other close friends to turn to, I rarely hear him mention anyone else.

"He's my friend Mum" Dylan states earnestly.

"I know darling but I just thought, you've got other friends too haven't you. We see a lot of Oliver and it might be nice to take one of your other mates instead perhaps?" I smile encouragingly.

"Don't you like Oliver?"

"I absolutely love him, I just thought you might want to take someone else, but no worries at all. *The Kid Who Would Be King* is on at one forty. We'll take Oliver to Pizza Express for lunch and then we'll go and see it yeah?"

"Yeah brilliant" Dylan joyfully replies.

I fire off a quick text to Emma asking if Oliver is free for us to take him out today. She replies almost immediately that he is. Dylan is already dressed and his hair looks neat, though I don't know if he's cleaned his teeth and so I query this.

"I was gonna' do it in a minute" he counters.

I take a cup of tea and a strawberry and yoghurt breakfast bar which I bought for Dylan but he declared "gross" upstairs to get ready.

I smile as I see another message icon next to the dating app:

'Yeah great thanks. Just having lunch with my sister and her twins.'

I send back 'Oh that sounds nice, how old are they?'

Right, jeans, slim leg but not skinny, plain white pumps, grey vest top, white open knit jumper. Whoever said batwing sleeves are out obviously didn't appreciate what they can do for the upper arms.

Pizza Express seems especially busy today. The ambient racket of kids laughing excitedly and Mums nattering charges the air. I can see The Blacksmith's Arms out of the window and try not to let it remind me of Tom. Or the tale of two Toms. Dylan, Oliver and I have ordered three large pizzas to share. The boys laugh and lark about whilst we await their arrival.

I don't want to keep looking at my phone but I'm itching to see if I've received another message from Pete. I savour the delicious feeling of contentment that caresses me when I see his name on my phone and the silly smile I've worn all day. The initial back and forth of fond messages when you first 'meet' somebody online. Before you meet up with them, if you do. Before you become too invested to recognise which way is up. Just two adults with the seed of an attraction, a bond, chatting. The hope of evenings snuggled up with box-sets, picnics in the park, footprints in the sand seemingly within your grasp. This is what I've craved.

I quite enjoyed the film. When I exit the cinema I am greeted by that familiar sense of slight disorientation which having been in the darkened cinematic cosmos seems to conjure.

While Dylan and Oliver chat vivaciously about the film and it's characters, I slip my hand into my bag and feel for my phone. Locating it's familiar shape, I depress the power button with my thumb, illuminating the screen. I see that there are two text messages, and one message on the dating app. The first of the messages is from a healthcare company I half-heartedly enquired about online a while ago, informing me of, to their credit, very reasonable monthly membership fees. The second is from Emma saying that, if the boys have been good, would

Dylan like to stay over at hers for the night? I save the message which I know will be from Pete for when I get home.

It's kind of Emma to offer to have Dylan overnight, I feel a bit bad as we've never had Oliver to stay at ours. If Dylan would like to stay over at Oliver's, then it'd be wonderful to curl up with a box-set or a good book, though I was looking forward to spending quality time with Dylan, where I'm not haranguing him to do his homework, eat his dinner or to put that day's pants into the laundry basket and not on the floor. The two of us eating chocolate and laughing together over a timeless comedy, *One Foot in the Grave* or something.

Predictably, Dylan is thrilled with Emma's suggestion of staying over.

"Right well lets go back home and get some overnight bits you'll need then" I say and so we drive home, the boys lost in an impassioned debate about which vehicle would be best to cross the desert over if one were having fireballs shot at them by the enemy, a Harley-Davidson or an armoured tank.

Back home, I pack a Sainsbury's bag with a clean pair of pyjamas, Dylan's toothbrush and toothpaste, clean underpants and a change of clothes. Shall I pack wellies? Will he need them? I think most of the mud has dried up now. Dylan excitedly asks me if he can take his Nintendo Switch, a plastic jar of dark blue slime, and some super hero figurines, all of which I say yes to.

"Don't forget to bring the charger back though if you do take that Nintendo thing" I say as I almost choked on my coffee when I learned how much my Mum paid for it.

Emma arrives bright eyed to collect the boys.

"Thank you, that's kind of you to have him over again. Here's a little something, it's not much" I say, handing her a scented candle. I bought several of them just after Christmas when they were going cheap with a view for them being Christmas presents for friends next year. This one is un-Christmasly named 'Spa Moments' and so I hope that's not obvious.

"Ah thank you" Emma grins. I don't know Emma well but her easy smile makes me suddenly want to.

I feel compelled to add "Maybe we could get a coffee soon?" and am rewarded with a dazzling beam, like a lighthouse searching for lost vessels.

"Yeah definitely, text me when you're free yeah?"

I nod emphatically and she throws her car keys up and caches them in a firm, jubilant grip. I'd like to try that but I know I'd probably drop them. The boys whirl out of the door, the prospect of fun awaiting them.

I resolve to work for an hour. Look at some student files and make some notes, then the evening is my own.

I suddenly remember the message from Pete and exhale with gratification as I sit at the table to read it.

"Yeah, I hardly see Karen as she lives in Sydney but is over at the moment staying with our parents. Oh they're so cute, Amelia and Logan, they're five. What are you up to this evening? Xx"

My thumbs hastily produce a reply, notifying him that I took my son and his friend out today and now have an evening to myself. After sending it however, I fret that it may have sounded as though I was available if he wanted to come round, like a cheap come on. I cringe inwardly.

Pete replies almost immediately:

'Do you think you'll try out a box-set? I'm really into *Ozark* at the moment. Xxx'

I like that he either didn't take my previous message the way I feared he might, or chose to not further any sleazy intent or naff flirting. I feel as though I'm talking to a real person, someone with a degree of substance and consideration.

I relax with a glass of Chardonnay and turn on the TV in the living room. It's the start of one of those *Come Dine With Me* marathons and so I pull a soft fleece blanket over myself, stretch out my legs and settle down to watch. I always think it's so rude the way strangers go rooting through each other's underwear drawers but maybe that's perfectly acceptable. As I absent mindedly watch the program, I enter into an enjoyable see-saw of messaging with Pete. We ask one another questions which I don't feel are probing, just interested.

I like the way he writes. I could of course be totally wide of the mark but he seems intelligent, kind, warm and interesting. I'm faintly aware of a small inner voice telling me not to invest too much, not to allow myself to become spellbound and then get hurt. But what's the alternative? Putting barriers up and holding people at arm's length? I'm glad that, after the past two weeks I'm still able to approach another connection with renewed wonder. I choose not to allow Tom to diminish my faith in human nature.

Of course, some people just want somebody to talk to, some lie and say they are single when they are married or in a relationship. But I find, after a couple of hours messaging with Pete a frisson of expectancy that he'll suggest meeting for a coffee, and sure enough, he does.

CHAPTER 18

It's possibly not the best idea, but we arrange to meet up. With the aid of laughing, smiling and cringing face emojis, I delicately inform Pete of my recent misadventures with somebody I met online, and, as a result, am looking for a connection with someone, but at a very slow place and initially wish to get to know them as a friend. Pete tells me what a relief this is as he wants to get to know someone 'organically' too and has had some disastrous dates himself.

A tingle of excitement chases through me as I get stuck into getting ready. I feel quite nervous, but tell myself that's just normal. If I'd never met Tom, I'd still get nervous meeting new people. Particularly a perspective love interest, its such a charged situation, expectations and hopes. Like a warped interview.

Pete lives in a coastal town about half an hour's drive away, so I suggest we meet there. It'll be nice to spend some time by the sea on a crisp early spring evening. Also, I don't want another first date knowing my address after the disastrous consequences with Tom. I'll be sufficiently removed from my stomping ground and thus feasibly feel safe. As though I can fold the situation away and put it into a high up cupboard should things not proceed to my liking. There won't be a constant reminder of it in my house and garden.

I do feel like this is a new beginning, a fresh start. As though a large ball of worry and fear has become dislodged and now I can dare to hope again.

I run a bath and select a nineties music channel on the TV in my bedroom. Oasis's *Wonderwall,* perfect getting ready music. I choose a maroon coloured eyeshadow, no eyeliner. I'm never completely sure how to apply highlighter so I ere on the side of caution and sweep a paltry amount onto my cheekbones, lest I resemble an extra from *Avatar.*

I opt for black leggings, a floral chiffon tunic and as its been a dry, sunny day, pointed black ballerina pumps embellished with small crystals. I dry my hair with the diffuser attachment, and spray into position what I hope resemble loose beach waves. Nude lip gloss, no perfume and out the door.

I've driven to the coast this way before with Dylan, though I still program the postcode of the bistro where we're meeting into the Sat Nav. I start the engine, it's fairly dark already so I need my lights, and set the radio. I think something happens in your late thirties where you no longer desire the same station as ten years before. Like a railway track changing signal, all previous muscle memory obliterated. I find myself wincing at Radio 1 and breathing a deep sigh of relief at Radio 2.

The bistro is down a slim, winding alley full of quirky shops and pop up art galleries. The exterior is lit by lanterns and has a warm, inviting feel. I'm ever so nervous, my palms are damp and my heart is pounding. Can I blow him out now? Say I was sick, no Dylan was. No I can't do that, it'd be inconsiderate and wrong. Do not pass go, do not collect £200. I take a deep, calming breath and enter.

My first though is that the entrance way is quite dusty, though in one of those 'quirky' manners, as though dusting is ridiculously beneath them and the dust has been strategically placed there by an up and coming young visionary. Easy chatter and laughter spills out as I open the door. I try and achieve a discreetly sweeping look to ascertain whether he's here already, from the area I can see, he doesn't appear to be.

"Hi!" exclaims buoyant young woman with long dark hair in a mid ponytail. "Table for two?"

"Hi, I'm um m meeting someone here, I don't know if they've arrived yet though."

"OK, no I don't think they have yet, no worries follow me."

Her natural confidence puts me at ease and I follow her, past white be-clothed tables into an L-shaped area of the dining room not immediately visible from the entrance. Is he here? As I crest the corner, I see there are around half a dozen tables, only one of which is occupied by two elderly gents. She seats me at one of those long velvet seats opposite a chair on a table for two. She asks if she can take my coat which I decline, but ask for a sparkling water.

I do the only reasonable thing a twenty first century person can do in such a situation, and pretend to be engrossed in the contents of my phone. Really I'm looking at some pictures of Dylan at Christmas.

"Hi, weren't waiting long were you?" a cheery male voice enquires. I look up to see a terrifically good looking man, vaguely reminiscent of the pictures on the dating app, but infinitely more arresting in person. Sparkling eyes and an effulgent, toothy smile like a young Marti Pellow.

"Hi, no not at all, just literally got here."

"Cool" he grins. "How are you?"

"Yeah good". I don't ask him back in case he turns out to be one of those people who feel obligated to give you chapter and verse minutiae of their day, which I don't think my nerves could stand. I opt instead, for neutral ground.

"How are you finding the world of online dating?" Oh fuck, did that sound frumpy and square? Like the head girl who never takes a library book back late.

"Yeah, good in general, has it's pitfalls, but I'm ever hopeful" Pete replies as he shrugs off his brick coloured jacket and hangs it on the back of the chair.

"Yes there are a few weirdos out there it seems" I say smiling coolly to indicate this comes from experience, but I'm totally OK with it which is ninety per cent true.

"Yeah so you went out with a guy and he turned into a stalker?"

"Well not a stalker exactly, but he caused me some unpleasantness."

Pete appears to consider this. "I once went on a date with a woman and get this – her husband came too!"

"What?" I say aghast, yet feeling instantly at ease with our shared stories of chagrin.

"Yeah, he just shook my hand and sat there quietly, just watching. Apparently it really turns him on!"

"No!"

Pete puts up his hands in mock surrender, "I kid you not."

"Blimey, what did you do? Did you stay?"

I stayed for a while, then did the whole "have to be up at six tomorrow" thing."

I laugh, appreciating Pete's good company. Though I'm well aware I thought this about Tom once.

"It's a shame actually as I really liked her" he adds wistfully.

"Her having a husband's a deal breaker though yeah?" I smile with raised eyebrows.

"I think so yeah" he smiles back.

We chat about TV shows, both classic and current. Turns out we both love *Peep Show* and *The League of Gentlemen.* When the waitress I saw before arrives to take our order, neither of us have even looked at the menu and hastily set about doing so. Pete enquires which beers they have and orders one. It's always a treat for me to eat good seafood so I order mussels with chorizo and lime which come with fries and freshly made crusty bread.

"I bet the fries come in one of those tiny silver buckets" I muse.

Pete laughs, "Yeah, or are stacked up like a game of Jenga."

The conversation flows effortlessly as we enjoy our meals. I'm insanely attracted to Pete yet I don't feel self conscious as a result, which I've found I can be.

It suddenly occurs to me, how did Tom get into my house? I'm certain he did. "No" a voice in my head chides me, I'm sitting here with a seemingly glorious man and I won't allow Tom to be the spectre at this feast.

I ask Pete about his job, he's a carpenter.

"Oh like Jesus" I say. "I don't know why I said that, I haven't had much sleep lately" I supply, feeling my face turning crimson.

Pete laughs good naturedly "Yeah I guess so. Don't know if he had a Black and Decker Powerfile though." He smiles with such genuine cheer and focus, that I know I made the right decision coming here to meet him.

We share a dessert, a chocolate profiterole ice cream sandwich. The pleasure of which is surpassed only by our forks accidentally touching throughout.

"Shall we go for a walk along the promenade?" I hear myself suggesting.

"Yeah lets do it. Have a walk I mean" and it gladdens me that he goes a bit red and seems to be as stumbling at this as I am.

Pete gently insists on getting the bill, "You get it next time" he offers.

We leave the bistro and wend our way through the narrow road. I'm faintly aware of some men laughing and smoking, but I care only about being close to Pete as we walk. I want dearly to hold his hand, I wonder if I'll get to one day. We head down a lowish hill towards the marina. Funny how a place looks and feels so different at differing times of the day. Small boats and a glimmering body of water are lit by twinkling lights, making them appear phosphorescent in the night air.

"What did you mean when you said 'no time wasters'?" I ask him.

"I don't know really. I just meant no one who'd mess me about and not be genuine."

"Wish I'd said that on my profile" I muse. "Do you think I'll have a boat here one day?"

"Absolutely" he says ardently. He smiles at me, "What would you call it?"

"Oh something really twee, like 'Inspiration'" I reply.

"Inspiration's quite a good name. Or if it's a yacht you could call it 'Aspiration' and rub it in us pauper's faces."

I laugh genuinely, "I'll have to remember that" I say.

I look at Pete, into his conker coloured eyes and I know he'll kiss me. Sure enough, I sense the slow progression of warm moistness as his lips tenderly cover mine.

It isn't a longing kiss, not totally. It's more a "I think you're great, please continue to be so" type kiss.

I ease away very slightly and smile. Pete smiles back at me, eye's twinkling. Magical as the moment is, I find I'm still a bit guarded underneath, in the next layer down.

"Thanks for a really wonderful evening" I tell Pete sincerely. "I'm so glad I came" I say with feeling, and squeeze his upper arm. "My car's just up there" I add by way of parting.

"I'll walk with you?" Pete offers uncertainly as if he's picked up on my reticence.

I take a deep breath and explain, "Well, when I went on a date with that other guy, we had a lovely first date too and then he walked me home. Then on the second date he was totally different, weird and insulting. So then I left and went home and he played some sort of pranks on me. So, lovely as you are and I've had such a nice time, I'm really quite reluctant to let anyone know my personal stuff like say, my registration number. I know it sounds mad, kind of silly, maybe precious, I don't know..." I can feel myself rambling but can't stop.

"Hey" Pete holds his arms out to me and I lean into them, it feels exquisite to be held. "That's completely understandable, and sensible. I'd be the same. Well done for coming out and meeting someone new when all that rubbish has been happening to you. Sorry if that sounded really patronising!"

I give a heartfelt half laugh "Not at all, it sounds wonderful." Pete's words sooth me but I'm as yet unable to totally trust in them.

"I'm just glad he didn't hurt you" Pete says holding me. "Right, get to your car and text me when you're home safely OK?"

"Roger that" I say playfully, but am actually so grateful for his easy empathy.

I have to stop myself skipping like a loony up the hill to my car. I get in but don't turn on the radio, my head is full to the brim with something as glorious as it is perilous – hope.

CHAPTER 19

I reach for the floral china jug of milk, the quiet murmur of conversations encompassing me. I really enjoy coming to the Historical Society meetings. The theme today is the Medici family, and as usual, Alan the group organiser has generously laid on tea, coffee and biscuits, my favourites, McVitie's dark chocolate digestives. It's nice to pour milk from a jug into a delicate china cup with a saucer. Evocative of a gentler time, when having tea was a more courtly affair.

"I've started seeing this guy" I tell Andy, glee shimmering off me.

"Cool, what's his name?"

"Pete" I reply slightly school-girlishly.

"So you've been and had a drink with him or just talking online?"

"Yeah met up with him a couple of times now."

"That's great" Andy says looking genuinely pleased for me. "Nice to see you smiling again" he adds.

"Yeah" I grin. "Hows everything with you?" I ask him

"Yeah pretty good, busy at work" He replies with a kind smile, though his eyes look a little sombre.

"Interesting about the Medicis isn't it, how they just took control like that. I'd love to have that sort of innate self belief."

"Yeah me too" he laughs.

"Right then, shall we talk about Cosimo's exile?" Alan's eagerness trumpets through the hushed mumblings and a motley crew of endearing people reassemble after their coffee break to imagine a time of renaissance Italy.

***

I eat my lunch in the staff room. Myself, Amy and two other teachers, Harry and Karen are chatting around two pushed together school tables.

"Just so soul crushing" laments Karen, "I asked them what they each wanted to be when they grew up and only three out of thirty one didn't want to be a vlogger or a you-tuber."

"I know," sighs Harry,"What's the point of teaching them linear functions if they know they can become set for life by appearing on 'Love Island.'"

The bell signifying the end of lunch, today also means that I only have an hour or so left of my school day as, every other Thursday I finish at two. Pete sent me a message earlier saying that he could probably slope off for a bit if I fancied a quick coffee before picking Dylan up and I've found it hard to think of anything else since.

After making some notes on students and how I think they are progressing, I pass the office, and through the main double doors into another resplendent day of sunshine.

I feel good, refreshed. Looking into my drivers mirror, I apply a little apricot lip gloss and give my hair a quick brush through with one of those tiny little brushes that usually come on a keyring. I
I'm meeting Pete in my town today, mainly for the sake of expediency, as we've not got long before I need to collect Dylan, but also because I can feel a frisson of trust growing inside me that

its safe to do so.

I enter the trendy new hipster cafe which allows vaping and see Pete immediately. He rises to greet me, an unveiled look of joy on his beguiling face.

"Hiya!" I say, so glad to see him.

"Hey baby, how was your day?" he asks hugging me.

I order a late and a small square flapjack containing dried cherries. It's fairly quiet in the cafe at the moment. Pete's eyes sparkle as he looks into mine and kisses my hand.

"Oh quite continental" a mixture of intense flattery and slight embarrassment compels me to offer.

"What?" he laughs gently.

"From the song. You know, 'Diamonds Are a Girl's Best Friend.'"

His eyes narrow playfully, "are you saying I need to put a ring on it?"

"Right, shall we stop saying the names of songs and chat about something else?" I ask in mock maturity.

"Yup. Um mm, how many songs can you think of in one minute with the word, um m 'Stop' in the title?

"What?" I groan exaggeratedly, "Oh I don't know"

"Come on your minute has started" he says ushering fourth suggestions with a theatrical roll of his hands.

I sigh, "OK, um mm, "Stop Right Now" by the Spice Girls..."

"That's just called "Stop" but I'll accept it" he teases.

"Can you interrupt me more, it helps me think" I tease back, suppressing a laugh. "Stop In The Name Of Love" by The Supremes, that's it".

"Hmm, paltry but passable" he surmises with a grin.

"Paltry but passable? Do you say that to all the girls?"

"Only the ones I really like" he answers, kissing my hand again.

I smile, "Nice day again" I point out as I glance out of a nearby window. A young woman pushing a buggy containing a contented, thumb sucking toddler walks past. A little boy, looks a lot like Dylan at that age I think to myself. By some cruel cosmic coincidence, a man walks past and at that exact moment looks into the window, his eyes meeting mine. God, it's him. Tom. I feel a bolt of anxiety shoot up my spine and cause my teeth to bite together, then in the same instant, I blankly look away from him and cover both of Pete's hands with mine. I think he's gone now, I feel myself relax again.

"You alright darling? Pete asks

"Yeah" I smile, "Right, how many song titles can you think of in one minute with the world 'don't' in?"

"Oh crikey" he exclaims, and begins to think.

The hour flies by far too quickly before I have to leave to collect Dylan. Outside the cafe, I'm unable or unwilling to resist; I encircle my arms around Pete's neck, kiss him lightly on the lips and hug him.

"You've got another text from Pete" Dylan informs me, padding into the kitchen where I'm draining some peas. "Your phone kept beeping in the bedroom when I was trying to play on my tablet in there."

"And why were you playing on it in my room?" I enquire of him in mock annoyance. I put my arms around his middle and kiss his head. "How was school sweetheart?

"Cool. Mr Miller says I should try out to be Sweeney Todd."

"Oh, are you going to put on a play?"

"Yeah, in term three. Which term is it now?"

"I honestly don't know darling. I should do shouldn't I?"

"Doesn't matter, I don't know either. So is Pete your boyfriend?"

"Not yet. Would you be OK if he did become my boyfriend?" I ask my son gently.

He shrugs, "I suppose so, if you want him to be."

"Well you've got a girlfriend haven't you, Millie."

"Oh she dumped me, Tamara's my girlfriend now" Dylan replies matter of factly.

"Oh right" I say, rolling my eyes and giggling.

 The icon shows I am in receipt of two text messages. The first from a local pizza place I ordered from once about six months ago who haven't stopped messaging me around once a week since. The other from Pete;

'Hey lady, how's your day been. Are you around to meet up tomorrow night? Xxxxxxxxxxxx'

I'm just about to reply that yes I am, when I suddenly remember I'm meeting Fiona tomorrow.

'Hey you, yes thanks was quite productive. I'm seeing how my friend Fiona tomorrow, but could do Wednesday? XxXx'

Dylan has karate after school on Wednesday and I'm sure Emma or my mum wouldn't mind having him for a couple of hours.

I run a bath, it's been lovely and sunny lately, but there's still a bit of a chill in the air, so I make it quite hot. Baths always feel indulgent for me as most of the time, I take showers. I pour in some of the posh bubble bath my Mum bought me for Christmas. That's weird, no bubbles are forming, when I've used it previously, a small amount has produced an abundance of them. I pour in some more, the same result. I look closer, I can't really determine because of the dim over mirror light which is serving to create a relaxing feel. I didn't want to be looking up at the main light.

I pull the cord for the main light which instantly swamps the space in a harsh yellow glare. But I can see quite clearly, it isn't white bath cream which is coming out of the bottle, but thin, transparent water.

But this came in a set from Boots, it's not something from a market or somewhere. What's happened? A dark shadow diminishes my recent gaiety somewhat. I don't know why, but I feel a little bit exposed, vulnerable. The feeling I had that day I discovered those images on my fence.

"OK" I say out loud to myself, "you said you were going to put all that fear and worry behind you. You've been doing so well." There is still a small niggling worry inside me, but I push it down, I choose to feel as I've been feeling lately, strong, confident and happy. I slide down into the bubble-less hot water and think about my next date with Pete.

CHAPTER 20

I park outside my mum's house, and pull my winter coat tighter around myself. It's sunny again but there's a real bite in the air. Mum's little black cat Tilly awakes from a nap in the garden and slinks up to me, butting her head against my shins affectionately. "Hello Tilly" I say, bending to stroke her sleek fur as she sidles around me. I let myself into mum's house which she always tells me to do.

"Hiya!" I call out as I wipe my feet on the door mat.

"Hi love!" Mum calls back chirpily. Though she lives alone, mum has adhered to set routines for years, and a fifties style primrose pink house coat is testament to a recent bout of cleaning. Bless her, I don't think you could buy those now.

Mum appears, beaming widely. "Go through love, I'll get the kettle on."

I envelop her in a hug and kiss her on the cheek, thinking she feels thinner than normal. I go into the cosy lounge and sit on the comfortable dun coloured fabric sofa. The TV is on and Noel Edmunds is asking a baffled looking woman if she has "actually done something very clever" on a rerun of *Deal Or No Deal.*

Mum roves into the lounge and sits on a matching armchair opposite. It almost devours her. "The trouble is, they're either too timid or too greedy" she surmises, looking at the screen.

"Difficult to know when's best though" I say, as I'm sure it is.

"Kettle's boiled" she declares, jumping up from the sofa again.

I wander into the be-pined kitchen, a spell of warm sun streaming through the windows making me smile.

"Need a hand at all?" I ask her.

"You can put these on a plate" she replies, handing me a packet of Fig Rolls, and one of Custard Creams, whilst seamlessly moving about the room.

"How are you?" I ask as I arrange the biscuits.

"Yes, good thanks. You? How's Dylan?"

I tell her that he is well, and happy at school.

"How's work?"

"Good, apart from seeing girls of like twelve obsessed with filtering photos of themselves, which they think makes them look better."

"What's that then?"

"Well, if you take a picture of yourself, your face, you can then make alterations to it." I sigh "It does upset me, seeing them making themselves look thinner, their lips bigger, teeth whiter, that sort of thing."

"Does it work for real? Can I have one?"

I laugh from my core, mum's down to earth, refreshing sense of humour is so therapeutic.

Mum and I watch the rest of the *Deal Or No Deal* episode, and then an old *Who Wants To Be A Millionaire?* Her general knowledge is as remarkable as mine is poor. She tells me how her garden is doing, and I tell her about Pete. I've never told mum about the nastiness that I suffered at the hands of Tom, only that we went out a couple of times but things didn't work out.

"I really like him and I'm seeing him tomorrow. We'll probably get some food and just chat. He's really easy to chat to" I smile.

"Does he make you laugh? Because that's important you know. I loved your father, but he didn't have a funny bone in his body. Apart from his hip obviously" she suppresses a giggle, eyes twinkling with fun. We both burst out in raucous laughter.

I nip into the large Morrisons on the way home. I'll get a few items, things we need now, before I go to Fiona's. I buy the food we need, plus washing powder and loo rolls, and a box of Thorntons chocolates for Fiona.

As I unlock the door and take everything into the house, I feel my phone buzz in my jeans pocket. It's a text message from Fiona;

'Hi hun, how are you? Would you mind if we hook up another day, I'm so tired. Xxx'

I type back; 'Hiya, no worries at all, do you need anything? Alright in yourself though are you? Not upset about that thing you told me before?" I know it sounds a bit covert, like a teenager wishing to claim their own secret dialogue, but I can't exactly write 'Brian' just in case, well, just in case.

I begin to put the food away when a reply arrives; 'I've decided to stay with the lovely one' followed by four blushing smiley emojis and two red hearts.

'Hey, that's brilliant. If you're sure then great' followed by three of the emojis with the broad smile, though not the smug looking grinning ones which I've noticed have recently been produced.

I know it's cheeky if not reckless, but even though we are meeting up tomorrow evening, I decide to ask Pete if he'd like to come over this afternoon for the couple of hours I was going to spend with Fiona. I don't want him to think I'm taking advantage because he's self employed, and I'll keep it light so he can always say 'no'. Besides, he originally asked if I was free this afternoon because he was. I hope he can, I really do.

I send him a text message; 'Hiya, how's your day going? Fiona doesn't feel very well now so... I wondered if you'd like to hang out with me for a couple of hours watching telly? XxXx'

'Hang out? I think the nineties want their phrases back XXXXX' followed by three laughing till they're crying emoji faces.

Another text message swiftly follows; 'Only joking sweetheart, I'd absolutely love to. You want me to bring anything? xxxx-xxx'

I love how light-hearted, childlike Pete is, he sort of allows me to see the funny side of things and I think that's just what I needed. I try to strike an equally light tone myself;

'Just your sexy self XxXx' adding an emoji with two red hearts for eyes.

Oh dear, should I have said the word 'sexy' is it too visceral? Will he think I'm going to answer the door in just high heels or something?

He sends back several of the bouquet of yellow and pink flower emojis.

At ten to one there is a knock on the door. I answer to a grinning Pete, his hair gorgeously mussed up and smelling of wood shavings.

"Ta-da!" he cries, producing two tubes of Pringles from behind his back.

"Memphis barbecue, which I'm sure used to be called Texas barbecue, and Screamin' Dill Pickle. I wonder if it does actually scream when you open the lid, like those ghost in a tins used to in the eighties."

I can't think of any words to describe how blissful I feel in this moment, so I throw my arms around him and kiss him ardently.

We curl up on the sofa with mugs of tea, tubes of Pringles, and each other. I feel so agreeable in his company, as though I can really let go and just enjoy the moment.

We decide to watch an episode of *Peep Show,* one we both love, the one with the narrow boat.
It feels glorious to snuggle into Pete and softly press my lips to the tender skin behind his ear, whilst laughing at the antics of Mark, Jez and Super Hans.

When the episode has finished, we chat for a while. Pete tells me about when he lived in Australia for two years, in Brisbane, and then right over the other side in Perth. I haven't travelled much, and am always fascinated by people who have.

"Yeah it was great, we had these lizards that lived under our house. I'll tell you what, they love Christmas out there."

"That's great" I smile. "Pete, you know I said I went out with that other guy twice, from the dating site?"

"Oh yeah" he replies, picking up on my sudden seriousness.

"Well, I mean I've got no actual proof, but he played these, pranks, games on me."

"Go on" Pete coaxes, his eyes narrowing in concern.

"I mean, it messes with your head, some of it I think I've imagined but, well there were horrific porn pictures, not photos, but pictures from a magazine, proper deviant stuff, stapled to my fence." I sigh, attempting to call to mind tangible examples rather than just the feeling I had of being watched which is hard to portray.

I continue, "There was a dead rat at the top of a cardboard recycling bin, which I know he put there to, well shock me I suppose. And the thing is, I'm pretty sure he's been in the house."

"When you weren't here you mean?" Pete's eyes widen in alarm.

"Yeah when I wasn't here. Just a feeling I've got. As though he's moved some of my stuff around or something, just little things. The thing is, I'm worried he'll come back."

"Shit. How many times do you think he's been here?"

"I honestly don't know. I'm not certain he has."

"When did you last see him?"

I take a deep breath into my cheeks then puff it out, "about three weeks ago."

"OK, well I mean if I was genuinely scared, as it looks like you are, I would go to the police. Also, I'd have the locks changed. In fact do that as soon as you can."

I nod, resolving to get onto it at some point tomorrow.

"I know that seems so obvious and I don't know why didn't do that before. I just haven't been thinking clearly lately is all".

"I'm not surprised, anyone would be the same. Sounds incredibly stressful." He opens his arms which I fall into, and as he holds me he says softly, "Don't worry, you've got me now."

CHAPTER 21

I see you've got your prince to protect you now. Sleigh all those nasty dragons. Who protects them though? When the beautiful princess and handsome prince live happily ever after, who protects the dragons? The wicked step mothers? The ugly sisters? Or the lone woodcutter who people quake at the sight of? Cast out because no one understands him. Only if you are understood can you be worth loving. Only if you fit their idea of what's understandable, have grown up tailored and conditioned to accept such espousal as a birthright. Can they smell something on him? Something from a long time ago, when he couldn't wield the axe? What is it? Piss? Blood? Burnt flesh? Fear? Despair?

CHAPTER 22

My school day passes smoothly on Wednesday. Years eight and nine were on a field trip to a Roman palace so it was pretty quiet. I do worry about online bullying now. Where the perpetrators are one step removed from the victim, its as though they have to be doubly as nasty in order to make up for it. They feel they need to impress a ready audience of baying spectators who need their blood thirst quenching, though deep down are probably horrified and just grateful it's not them. We've already given letters, emails, and regular assemblies about bullying through social media and how we will not tolerate it.

I arrive home at just gone four today, filled with excitement about seeing Pete again. We've made a reservation at a fish restaurant about half an hour's drive from here. A part of me worries that I've not known Pete long, yet here I am getting a bit silly and fantasising about us being together. It just feels so decadent to spend time with him, particularly now the evenings are starting to draw out more. Perhaps I'll rein back my feelings to a gentle trot and not the gallop they usually turn into. The old sayings from a bygone era come to mind, be a bit come hither, don't put all your eggs into one basket. It seems human beings have always grappled with similar emotions, despite what style of dress they wear or who's on the throne.

Mum is collecting Dylan after karate and giving him dinner at hers. They'll be back around eight. Pete is picking me up for the date at half past five, so I've plenty of time to get ready.

I know exactly how I like tea, the teabag not in too long, though long enough. I prepare two white slices of toast with butter and chocolate spread; shock horror I smile to myself as I think of all the tutting from some women my age who live on air.

I put 'Now 90's' on my TV, though it's quite dancey and I feel I'd like to chill out a bit. Enjoy the ritual of getting ready. I select 'Classic FM' on the radio channels and sigh with fulfilment as some Bach drifts through the room.

I decide to go the whole hog - maroon coloured eyeshadow, eyeliner and mascara, as a two finger salute to Tom. I'm pleased I've managed to expunge him and his cruelty from my life, I feel sorry for anyone else he meets though. Maybe I should start a website where we post details of people who are completely unreasonable and downright nasty. Though I know people would only abuse it and put perfectly decent people on there just to get back at them. Human nature is a double edged sword, incredibly kind, shockingly dark.

Although I own a few, I don't generally wear skirts or dresses. I think I'll choose some black trousers which have a tailored look about them and a black top with delicate lace sleeves. I put on the necklace Keith bought me, and go for some fine silver hoop earrings. I don't have any rings or bracelets as they'd just become an anxiety toy with which id fiddle all the time. Hair just down and loose, smart black ankle boots, dab of Coco Mademoiselle.

I channel surf for a minute to find something to watch whilst I'm waiting for Pete. I like *The Chase*, though I shan't watch it as quiz shows always frustrate me when the contestant doesn't know the answer. Not that I often do. I arrive at a *Judge Judy*, and settle down among the pillows to wait.

At half past five on the nose, there is a knock at the door. I answer it to find Pete standing a little back from the entrance, but smiling expansively.

"Hiya!" I exclaim, so glad to see him.

"Hey lady, how was your day?" he asks kissing me on the cheek.

Its so lovely to rest my head on Pete's shoulder as he drives. He smells heavenly, like walking into a portal where everything is made of fresh wood of all different types. From the darkest ebony, to the reddest mahogany, to the palest ash. I kiss his shoulder and snuggle into him more. He kisses my head and I'm so pleased I gave the dating site another try.

Pete tells me about the two guys he works with. Terry, who started the business and manages the paperwork, and Garry, his son who works on the commissions with Pete. They are currently repairing some beams in a church.

"It's so beautiful, stone, I love stone as well. Yeah we repair stuff, and make stuff I guess" he says affably with the ease of somebody truly contented in their work. He tells me how nice it is to work with Garry and Terry, and I think to myself how pleasant it is to hear a person speak so respectfully about others, without even the temptation of a little dig.

"Great to construct things," I say, as though sprinkled with some of the magic of his lively energy. "I mean, to see a piece of wood and know how it would look as a chair or something."

"Well I mean, when you see a troubled youngster, you can see how you can help them become happier. Must be so rewarding."

"It really is, has its moments though I can tell you."

"If their problems were easy to solve, they wouldn't have them in the first place" he shrugs.

"True" I smile. "Hey, we both shape natural things" I say.

"I'm the only one who gets splinters though" says Pete, turning to smile at me.

"I've been lashed out at" I inform him.

"No way!"

"Yeah, a couple of times." I attempt to lighten the mood a bit "Talking of re-shaping things, I lost over two stone last year."

"Hey, well done honey" he replies. "Not easy to do, I'd have liked you then anyway though."

"You old charmer" I jokingly chide him.

He laughs and removes his hand from the gear stick to squeeze mine.

The restaurant is in a quiet road behind some old fisherman's huts. The air is brimming with the fresh aroma of the ocean.

"Right, I think it's just round past these huts" Pete states whilst reaching back his hand to take mine, a movement I hope will become second nature.

The restaurant is vast, there must be forty tables. Though somehow, it seems cosy. The winsome chintziness making me feel as though I'm visiting my favourite aunt.

We sit by a large window. I'm pleased to see some chalky clifftop flowers are arranged charmingly in a slim porcelain vase. As Pete lowers himself to the chair, I see him run a reverent hand over the naked wood of the table. I love how we both notice beauty in the world.

I order chargrilled squid which I've never tried before. I take both of Pete's hands in my own. He lifts the tangle of hands and kisses mine. He really is so lovely.

We chat about places we'd both like to visit and things we'd like to do if we could. He has such an adventurous and endearing way of seeing things.

We leave the restaurant hand in hand and walk back leisurely to

Pete's car.

On the drive home we listen to the radio and are both gratified to hear a succession of nineties tunes which we sing along to.

"Savage Garden - Truly, Madly, Deeply. Nineteen ninety, hmm m nine?" Pete states triumphantly.

I chuckle, "Eight."

"How do you know?" Pete asks impressively.

"I just love music" I offer, "I knew I loved you before I met you" I add quietly.

"What?" Says Pete

"Another song by them" I say, and can actually feel my eyes twinkling.

I love coming into my town, I feel so at home here. I left to go to uni but I'm glad I came back again to be near my mum. I have some great friends here and it really feels like home.

"Would you mind if we just stopped off at Sainsbury's?" I say. "I've suddenly remembered I haven't got any milk left and when mum drops Dylan back, I'll want to start settling him down for bed."

"Sure, no problem" Pete replies graciously.

"Thanks hun. Do you need anything?"

"Nope, I'm good thanks."

I get out of the car and nip over the road. Its colder again now.

The light seems quite harsh in the shop, compared to the intimacy of the restaurant and Pete's car. I walk past the flowers, the fruit and vegetables, and along past the tins until I reach the chiller. I take a two pint green out and head towards the checkout. Do we need toothpaste? I think we probably do. I remember when there were two or three types. It seems there's about fifty now. I select something which I hope will accommodate all our oral care needs and continue to the checkout.

"Hiya, you're Dylan's mum aren't you?" The smiling, auburn haired lady asks me.

"Hi, yes I am" I reply.

"Yeah I thought so. I'm Kate; Annie's mum" she offers.

"Oh OK. I'm Bethan."

"How's Dylan getting on?" she asks.

"Yes well thanks. He loves Mr Miller."

"Oh he's just great isn't he" she beams.

"Definitely. Is Annie looking forward to the play?"

"Oh she wont stop talking about it."

"No Dylan neither, have you any other children?"

"Yes, an older boy, Thomas. Mr Miller taught him too."

"Oh OK, we're lucky to have him as a teacher aren't we. Well I'll see you around then Kate" I smile.

"Yeah you too" Kate smiles back.

I quickly cross the road to the car. I love Pete's daft sense of humour. I can see him, comically pretending to be asleep, head back on the rest, jaw slack, as though I took such a long time.

I smile and shake my head. "Yeah yeah" I groan as I sit down in the passenger seat.

"Lovely lady in there. Mum of one of the kids in Dylan's class. I suppose I should make more of an effort to get to know the other Mums."

Pete doesn't stir and is still pretending to be out for the count.

"Very funny" I say gently elbowing him. "Lets go then."

I look over at him. My face falls. I hear myself let out a noise, what the fuck? No, it's not real, it can't be. What's happening?

A line like a bolt of lightning runs across the milky skin of Pete's neck. His throat has been cut.

PART TWO

CHAPTER 23

DI Nicky Cosgrove stretches out her arms and back. It had been another tense night last night. She and her wife Julia are looking to adopt a baby, but recently achieving the rank of Inspector meant that Nicky worked long and erratic hours, and seemed to spend less and less time at home. Nicky has reached the title through dogged hard work and determination, no fast tracking for her. She loves her wife, and she loves her job. Giving the necessary attention to both however, can be a very precarious balance. People who are not on the force can't always comprehend its demands. Simply put, you marry a copper, you marry the job as well.

Nicky would dearly love to have a family with Julia. A precious little bundle she could shower with all the love and attention every child should receive. Ironically, if anyone knows how important a safe, loving home is to a child, it would be Nicky. The number of clever, bright kids she's seen lose their health, liberty, or even lives to drugs, crime and violent relationships. In different situations, i.e. a parent figure who actually gave a shit about them and nurtured and guided them to become happy, confident individuals, well, she'd see far fewer.

It frustrates Nicky. Of course she'd love to take in a baby or child and love it forever, seeing him or her flourish into adulthood. As an orphan herself now, Nicky understands the crippling feeling of loneliness and would be honoured to protect a little human being from the darkness of that.

Julia is one of those people who can light up a room, charismatic, magnetic. But she can also be so irrational and hot-headed when Nicky is tired and simply wants to talk things over calmly. Julia works from home writing articles for a series of culinary magazines and can largely pick and choose her hours.

Nicky's Mum and Dad were both coppers. They'd be so very proud of her she thinks to herself, half a smile and half a choked back sob battling to be the dominant emotion. Her Dad George reached DI and loved it, turning down subsequent offers of promotion for the rest of his career. He always believed in Nicky, championed her every decision with complete conviction.

Nicky remembers her mum, Philippa telling her about how hard it was being a female police officer in the eighties and nineties. How spiteful discrimination and blatant sexual harassment were commonplace, and were simply seen as par for the course for a woman absurd enough to believe she could help fight crime.

It beggars belief now to think that, in the eighties, women police officers were given a handbag with a truncheon that was sufficiently small enough to fit inside it as part of their uniform.

Nicky is extremely proud that courageous women like her mum paved the way for the women of today to be as accepted within the force as their male counterparts. Indeed, it is now recognised that female officers can often have a much more calming effect on a volatile situation than male ones. Men instinctively want to lash out at other men, and much less so when faced with a woman. Women police officers are also less likely to use excessive force, instead using verbal skills to deal with volatile situations.

It's been two years now, well twenty months, three weeks and one day since George, Philippa and their beloved Labrador, Biscuit perished in a car accident, whilst en route home from a walking holiday in Devon.

Nicky sighs and continues filling in the Police Report; detail of event, action taken and summery.

Nicky stands as she suddenly sees DS Dan Sheppard urgently approaching her, a distressed set to his mouth.

"Dan?" Nicky asks, concerned.

"Gov, a man's been murdered in Elmsfield. A woman just called it in."

"Elmsfield? Fuck."

"I know." Elmsfield is a sleepy market town nearby and, other than a few domestics and a spate of break-ins a while ago, it's rarely visited by the police much less CID.

Nicky climbs into the passenger side of the black Audi A4 saloon, she likes Dan to drive. It's an agreeable arrangement the pair have naturally fallen into in their eight months of working together.

As they drive into the town, it seems eerily quiet. The Indian restaurant looks empty, no youngsters hanging around the bus shelters. This however, is rapidly juxtaposed to the scene which greets them as they turn at the mini roundabout towards the small Sainsbury's Local.

Two uniformed patrol officers stand beside a distraught looking woman. One of the officers is forcefully telling a sizeable group of onlookers to move back.

Dan smoothly parks beside the patrol car. Nicky gets out, it's a chilly evening. It also contains the fizz she recognises from previous crime scenes. Acute fear and perverse excitement. As the Senior Investigating Officer it will be her job to collect as much information as possible at this early stage. Questioning victims and witnesses with a calm detachment, and trusting her gut instincts.

Most of the crowd begin to dissipate. There's always a few rubberneckers who love watching this sort of thing.

Nicky approaches the constables and the woman.

"Ma'am, this is Bethan Archer who called in the incident" one of the officers, a woman with cinnamon skin and freckles peppered around a petite nose informs Nicky.

"OK thank you" Nicky replies.

The woman, Bethan, looks to be in her mid to late thirties. Of slimmish build, dressed as one would to go out for the evening. Smart black trousers and boots, a black winter over coat, silver hoop earrings and mid-length toffee coloured hair. She's in shock, holding her stomach as though she's been punched. Legs bent slightly, back slumped forward, her body trying desperately to uphold her.

Dan, who has been talking on the phone, jogs across the road towards Nicky.

"SOCO are on their way Gov" he informs her.

Scene of crime officers will now preserve and gather evidence. In the meantime, Nicky and Dan must assess and coordinate the situation at hand, removing any potential threats to themselves or any members of the public, administering and arranging first aid to anyone at the scene who should be in need of it, and organising jobs for other police officers and people who work for the police.

Nicky speaks to Bethan who looks utterly distraught.

"Bethan, I'm DI Nicky Cosgrove. Can you tell me what happened here?" Nicky asks in a gentle yet authoritative voice.

Bethan gasps, looks up at Nicky, her eyes abnormally large, lost. "I've got to call my mum" she replies in a quiet, slightly stammering voice.

"Why have you got to call your mum, Bethan?"

"My son, Dylan. He's ten. He was staying, has been staying, no not staying..."

"Take a deep breath."

Bethan attempts to take in a deep breath. Although she can only manage short one s currently, she does appear to be slightly calmer and more collected.

"My son, I've been on a date tonight, went out with Pete. My mum's been looking after Dylan, she'll be bringing him back to my house soon, or now- I'm not sure what the time is. She'll be wondering where I am. She'll be worried."

"You were out on a date this evening with the man in the car?" Nicky looks over at him "your mum was looking after Dylan at her house and is bringing him back to yours?"

"Yeah" Bethan says, appearing to struggle for breath again.

"Can you make arrangements for Dylan to stay over at your mum's tonight Bethan?"

"Yeah. OK yeah."

"OK, lets come and sit in my car. You can call her then."

Nicky takes Bethan's elbow in a guiding hand and leads her across the road to the Audi. Bethan is breathing through her mouth, still in shock though allowing herself to be lead. Nicky can hear Dan's voice behind her, arranging for the crime scene to be guarded whilst SOCO arrive.

Nicky opens the back door, and Bethan gets in. Nicky's statuesque form then walks calmly to the other side of the vehicle and climbs in next to Bethan.

The interior has those plasticky type seats. It's warm and smells of some sort of cleaning fluid. Bethan is grateful for the warmth, she was shivering a bit.

"Call her now from your phone Bethan" Nicky gently instructs her.

Bethan logs into recent calls, locates 'Mum' then presses the call button.

"Hi Mum! I got the part of Sweeney Todd!" exclaims an excitable Dylan. "He cuts people's throats, can you imagine that!"

Bethan closes her eyes tightly, her jaws pressing together. She sighs slightly before responding.

"That's wonderful sweetheart, could I speak to Nan please?"

"Yep, I'll just get her for you. Bye Mum."

A tear runs down Bethan's cheek.

"Bethan?" her mother's voice is soothing.

"Hi Mum, um m look, something's happened, I need you to have Dylan for me tonight. I know he hasn't got any of his things. Could you nip to mine and fetch his toothbrush, pyjamas and that?"

"Don't need to love. He's got all that stuff here as well. Is everything alright?"

Bethan sighs again, for longer this time. "No not really." She can sense Nicky's cool gaze and feels she is being silently implored not to speak about Pete dying. Being killed. Is he dead? of course he is. Why....... Bethan takes a calming breath, she doesn't want to worry her mum any way.

"Yes there's been a bit of a problem", Bethan musters a more business-like tone as she can't think of any other way in which to deal with things. "If Dylan could stay with you...."

"Of course he can."

"Could you take him to school tomorrow?"

"Absolutely, I'll have him for however long you need. If you need anything at all, you must phone."

Bethan exhales, "thanks Mum, I appreciate it." And ends the call.

"Bethan this is DS Sheppard. Bethan here called in the incident DS Sheppard."

Bethan vaguely registers that someone else has climbed into the car, into the drivers seat. A man. He smiles kindly, "Hello Bethan" he says.

"Now" continues Nicky, "can you tell us what happened Bethan?"

CHAPTER 24

"I thought he was joking about as he had a sort of goofy sense of humour. Then I saw the wound and realised his throat had been cut. Why wasn't there more blood? Can it really have happened in the time I was in Sainsbury's?" Bethan finishes relaying the evening's events to Nicky. She looks down at her intertwined fingers and clasps them together.

"OK, so Dylan's safe with your mum for the night. Now we're going to go to the station for you to give us a formal statement" Nicky says markedly. "Can you do that Bethan? We need to ask you some more questions."

Bethan looks straight at Nicky "yes" she replies.

They arrive at the police station in the next town. A genteel Victorian building with a touch of the Gothic style about it. For a blissfully reprieving moment, Bethan thinks to herself that the yellow sandstone facade looks beautiful in the moonlight. As though the moon is playing a projection of dancing shadows over the building to cheer her up. Pete would have thought it was beautiful too, he noticed things like that. It doesn't work for long though, a feeling of emptiness quickly follows, saturating her very being.

There is nobody outside the police station and the vicinity seems very quiet. Nicky holds open the main door for Bethan to enter the building and leads her past an empty reception area, along a corridor with a dark blue floor.

"OK, come in here Bethan. Would you like some tea or coffee?"

Nicky opens a grey door marked 'Interview Room 2'.

"No. Can I have some water please?"

"I'll get that Bethan" says the man, DS Sheppard in a friendly voice.

Nicky switches on the lights which suffuse the room with harsh, too bright light.

"Right, I'll be back in a minute Bethan OK?" Nicky says matter-of-factly, then with a small smile, leaves the room.

The room is sparsely furnished with just a grey office type table, around which four red plastic tub chairs are screwed to the floor. Alone with her thoughts, Bethan suddenly feels a curious mixture of heightened fear and extreme fatigue. Like one of those nightmares where you're trying to run away from something but your legs are leaden and any progress you make is excruciatingly sluggish.

It's quite stuffy in the room, as if a radiator has been turned up to the highest setting. She still doesn't want to take off her coat though. The familiarity of it's feel offering comfort.

The door opens and the two officers, DI Nicky Cosgrove and DS Dan Sheppard re-enter. Both have shed their coats. DS Sheppard puts a plastic cup of water gently down in front of Bethan.

"Thank you" she says in a small, rusty voice.

"Now, we're going to try to work out exactly what happened this evening OK Bethan?" Nicky says.

"Um m, do I need a solicitor?" Bethan asks anxiously.

"No, at this stage, we'll just be asking you some questions and try to get a clearer picture of the evening's events" Nicky replies with her customary crispness.

"So you left the car and Mr Gadsall was alive?" asks DS Sheppard.

"Pete? Was that his surname? I didn't know that" replies Bethan looking down, her voice full of sadness. "Yes, I was in Pete's car with him and he was fine. I needed to duck into Sainsbury's quickly as I just needed some milk. I was in there, I don't know fifteen, twenty minutes I suppose. When I got back to the car, I honestly thought Pete was larking about as he did that. Then I saw a mark on his throat and realised what had happened." Bethan sighs deeply as though this revelation has extracted all of her energy.

"It took you twenty minutes to buy some milk?" asks DI Cosgrove sceptically.

"Well I initially only went in for milk, then I looked at the toothpastes for a while and chose one. Then I got talking to the lady at the checkout. She recognised me from the school and said she was a mum there too.

DI Cosgrove writes something down. "She served you?"

"Yes."

"What's her name?" asks DS Sheppard?

"Um m Kate I think. Yes Kate. I hadn't seen her before but she asked me if I was Dylan's mum." Bethan registers that she's nervously rambling.

"OK, we'll check that out" DI Cosgrove informs Bethan and nods to DS Sheppard who then leaves the room.

"So you returned to the car?" DI Cosgrove continues writing.

"Yes. I left Sainsbury's, crossed over the road and saw Pete with his head back. I thought he was joking because I took a bit longer than I said perhaps? Like joking that I was ages and he'd fallen asleep as a result. Seems silly now."

"No, it's OK. Just say what happened."

"I looked over at him, across and that's when I noticed the mark on his throat." Bethan looks depleted. The initial adrenalin which fills your system when faced with a dangerous situation appears to be wearing off. She looks exhausted.

"Did you try to resuscitate Pete at all Bethan? Check for a pulse?"

"No. I called the police immediately. Should I have called an ambulance? Oh God!" Bethan slumps down in the chair, tears falling out of her. Nicky feels a rush of sympathy for her.

The magnitude of the situation is really kicking in now, Bethan is crying anxiously.

"Do you want to stop for a minute Bethan? We could have a couple of minutes break if you like?"

"Yes please" Bethan answers gratefully. "Can I get a tissue out of my bag?"

"Of course" replies DI Cosgrove.

Bethan reaches into her bag and feels around for a packet of tissues she's sure is in there. Locating it, she fishes one out with a slightly shaking hand and blows her nose.

"I called 999 as soon as I realised. I didn't check for a pulse or anything like that as it didn't occur to me."

"OK, thank you Bethan, that's helpful. It's important for me to know exactly what happened and when."

"OK."

The door opens and the affable DS Sheppard appears. He smiles kindly at Bethan and whispers something into DI Cosgrove's ear. She nods and makes a noise in agreement with whatever he's telling her.

"OK Bethan, now I'd like you to fill in this form" DI Cosgrove removes a crisp piece of white A4 paper from a burgundy paper folder which has lain under the paper on which she was writing. She fills out some details and passes it to Bethan.

Bethan tentatively takes the proffered form and looks at it. It is entitled 'Witness Statement.' She can see where DI Cosgrove has written under the section marked 'Officer' and is surprised to see that the stately detective's hand writing is not the perfect script she'd imagined, but rather rushed and messy looking.

Bethan fills out the sections 'Name', 'Address', 'Date', 'Occupation', and records once again the events of the evening as she saw them.

She passes it back to DI Cosgrove. She's so tired. If they're going to charge her with Pete's murder, she half wishes they'd just throw her into a cell and be done with it, at least she'd be able to get some sleep.

"OK Bethan, thanks for that. If you could just sign here for me" DI Cosgrove indicates the area with a sloppy asterisk.

Bethan signs the paper bleakly.

"Right Bethan, I just need to have a word with DS Sheppard OK?"

"OK" Bethan replies softly.

The two detectives leave the room. Bethan tries to take some deep, calming breaths, but they make her feel even more nervous.

An idea comes to her. A trick she used to employ in the children's home or whenever she knew in her heart she was going there again. A coping strategy she invented. It's where you close your eyes, cuddle into your coat, and imagine you're on a warm beach somewhere exotic. Warm and safe with no-one around. Bethan remembers this trick working every time, melting her fears away. She tries it now, tries hard. It doesn't work.

CHAPTER 25

The detectives Sheppard and Cosgrove come back into the room along with a uniformed constable.

"Right Bethan, we've learnt some more about what happened. Thanks to some CCTV we've seen you in Sainsbury's and like I say, learnt some more about what happened." DI Cosgrove assumes her previous seat at the table. DS Sheppard sits back down beside her. The uniformed constable remains standing solemnly by the door, hands behind his back, like a soldier, or a footman from another era.

"You saw who did it? Who murdered Pete?" Bethan's eyes widen and brim over with tears.

"We can't discuss that I'm afraid" says DI Cosgrove with a touch more humility. She looks into Bethan's eyes, "Bethan, did you see anyone at all hanging around? A person on their own or with a group?"

"No, I honestly didn't. I mean, I wasn't looking but I certainly didn't notice anyone. I mean, there's groups of teenagers around Elmsfield as there would be everywhere, but I've never known of anyone carrying a weapon and killing someone! I've never even seen a dead person before. Did they want his money?" Bethan squeezes her eyes together, tears spill down her cheeks. Her anguished pain is obvious.

"Do you know of anyone who would want to harm Pete in any way?" DS Sheppard asks, his voice soothing.

"No, absolutely not. I haven't known Pete long, and we don't have any shared friends that I can think of. I don't know any of his family. He only told me about some guys he works with, a father and son I think it was, just that he really enjoyed working with them and the sort of things they made and that. I honestly don't know". The feelings coursing through Bethan are horribly real, yet the whole situation feels completely removed from reality. The reality she thought she knew.

Nicky feels for Bethan, the woman is utterly broken and Nicky can see the genuine surprise and confusion in her eyes. The person she and DS Sheppard have just seen on footage from a CCTV camera outside a block of apartments, opposite Sainsbury's clearly shows Pete in his car, parked outside, opposite Sainsbury's. Bethan is seen getting out of the vehicle, and then subsequently, on CCTV from inside the Sainsbury's Local supermarket, buying things and appearing to chat with Kate Gardner who works there, just as she said.

The person they clearly saw walk briskly up to Pete is not Bethan. Tall, wearing dark tracksuit bottoms, and a parka type coat with the hood up, opening the driver's door and very efficiently pushing their right arm into the car, toward Pete's neck. Without much of a struggle, probably because of the shock, Pete's head can be clearly seen falling back, his hand rising up with the fingers splayed. The hooded person then shuts the door and without looking around, walks briskly away. As though they had been asking for directions or the time.

It wasn't a chance encounter, Pete wasn't in the wrong place at the wrong time, this was personal. Of that Nicky is sure. It's possible Bethan knows this character, It's possible they were in it together and she planned the whole thing or was complicit in the planning. Maybe she doesn't know them and it's somebody Pete upset. Nicky will have to get a team to look into his past, perhaps there could be a spurned lover, ex partner or wife. Nicky's gut is telling her that Bethan had nothing to do with this. That she was, as she says on a date with Pete, nipped into a shop and came out to find him murdered.

None the less, Nicky now has no choice but to arrest Bethan, seize her belongings and telephone, and search her home, emails and internet history for any mention of a plan for a joint enterprise.

CHAPTER 26

Nicky, sighs, she can see Bethan through the perspex window in the door, sitting at the table in the interview room. It's plain that the poor thing is overwrought with hurt and shock. Nicky's human instinct wants to protect Bethan from any further distress. Nicky sighs again, runs her hand through her thick, chestnut hair.

Both Nicky and Dan are pretty sure Bethan wasn't complicit in Pete being so brutally yet casually murdered. Each of the detectives know they shouldn't particularly believe Bethan to be innocent before she's actually proven to be so, but gut feelings can count for a lot in policing. And how can you, in all good conscience, make a broken person feel even worse?

"If she did know, and arranged it, she's a bloody good actress" Dan remarks.

Nicky thinks of the chilling CCTV footage she and Dan have seen of a very clean extinguishing of a human life. Though the murder occurred in the late evening, it was in a public place, opposite a busy shop and the weather had been fine. The perpetrator did not seem in the least dissuaded by any of these factors. Also, if it had been a professional execution, why did the murderer not realise they were directly under the gaze of a security camera, the footage of which the police would surely be able to recover very quickly?

Did they want to be caught? Did they care? It doesn't really make sense. Rather like attempting to put together a ten thousand piece jigsaw when all you can see are dozens and dozens of little pieces, some related and some not.

"Well, on the other hand, maybe she's so upset because she did know and didn't actually believe it was going to happen. I mean now it actually has she can't accept or believe it."

Dan looks at Nicky sceptically. He can see she doesn't really believe such a theory at this point.

Nicky puts her hands up in mock surrender "Just playing devil's advocate" she tells him.

"I know" Dan says smiling at her, "Maybe that is what happened" he offers, shrugging, "Or someone could have something on her and she feels she can't tell anyone. Maybe something to do with her kid or her mother?

"Yes maybe" Nicky muses quietly. Though these possibilities seem unlikely, Dan and Nicky cannot ever assume to rule them out. They've both seen too much of the very depths of human murk.

"We'll have to check her home and question her her associates then" Nicky tells Dan in a hushed tone as the two of them look in at Bethan from outside the door. Nicky's usually professional tone now edged with regret.

"Yep" Dan nods, his expression subdued.

"Right, lets make this as painless as possible" says Nicky. The thought of doing everything which needs to be done as swiftly as they can to prevent any further pain for Bethan galvanising them both into action.

Dan and Nicky re-enter the interview room and sit back down at the table, opposite Bethan.

"Hi Bethan. Now this is just procedure OK. But with the new evidence that we have now, we need to check to see if you were aware of, or complicit in anything relating in what happened to

Mr Gadsall under the joint enterprise law.

"What?" Bethan looks crestfallen.

"It's just procedure Bethan" Dan explains gently, "we need to ascertain if you were previously aware of what was going to happen tonight."

"Of course I wasn't!" Bethan's voice has become slightly horse. In the last hour, deep furrows of despair have carved themselves into her face. As though her insides cannot contain any more anguish.

"It's honestly just routine" Dan says, trying for a matter of fact tone.

"Bethan Archer, I am arresting you on suspicion of soliciting to murder. You do not have to say anything, but it may harm your defence if you do not mention, when questioned, something which you later rely on in court." Nicky looks straight at Bethan.

"What? Why?" It genuinely hurts Nicky to see Bethan's bewildered, frightened face. Nicky hardens her resolve and leads Bethan through the door of the interview room, and back down the blue floored corridor.

"My mum, I'm entitled to a phone call aren't I?" Bethan turns between Dan and Nicky, looking hopefully at both.

"I'll call your mum Bethan, don't worry" Dan informs Bethan softly.

Nicky leads Bethan to the desk at the main entrance. A shortish lady with brassy yellow hair under a police officer's hat and a ruddy pink complexion smiles tightly at Bethan. The lady's slate grey eyes have a disappointed look to them.

Bethan faintly registers the lady talking to her, telling her things. Bethan feels so very tired and overwhelmed that she doesn't take any of it in. Something about the right to free legal advice, telling somebody where you are, and medical help if you are feeling ill. Bethan does feel ill, she feels sick. Sick and dizzy and in utter disbelief that all this is happening.

The lady escorts Bethan down a further corridor, off to the left, not immediately visible from the reception desk. Bethan doesn't know what to think. There was no one here earlier. Now this strange little lady is leading her further, deeper into this hellish nightmare. The corridor seems to be getting thinner, closing in on itself. The lighting feels more focused, like a spotlight. The colours are too bright, garish, jarring. Bethan feels as though she's inside some kind of dystopian film by Stanley Kubrick. What the hell is happening now?

CHAPTER 27

Bethan sits with her head in her hands. She has had her photograph taken, given finger prints and had to hand in her bag, phone, earrings, and the necklace Keith bought her to that lady, Lesley, who placed them carefully into a see through bag.

Bethan sighs and looks around her. The walls of the police cell are tiled in an off white, off yellow, off peach, off everything type colour. Vile grey grout between them. She sits on the bed, the wooden block frame of which is around six and a half feet in length. The bed is topped with a royal blue PVC plastic mattress from which the accompanying pillow has obviously been cut. If you were to align the two together, they would both slot into the frame perfectly. With the pillow on top of the pancake thin mattress, a gap of around ten inches is revealed at the foot of the bed. Bethan doesn't mind, she can't lay down anyway.

Behind the bed is a small space created by a partition wall, in which nestles a metal toilet and basin. Both have obviously been cleaned, though the vague scent of other people's urine still hangs quite pungently in the air.

Rather strangely, a metal box in the wall which looks like it's purpose is to contain toilet tissue, but is quite bereft of any, is located around the opposite side of the partition, by the cell door. In the top third of the wall above the bed, is a barred window.

Maybe she's not here, maybe she's at home asleep in her big, soft bed and this is all just a bad dream. But she knows it's real. Crazy but real. That mark on Pete's neck, somebody inflicted that.

Poor, sweet, wonderful Pete. If only he were here. If only he could be here to hold her, stroke her hair, kiss her fears away.

A sharp rap at the cell door startles Bethan. The sound of a lock clicking is followed by Lesley entering the cell, followed by a diminutive man of around sixty who looks as though he were conjured by a children's illustrator.

"Bethan, this is the duty solicitor, Aleister Asquith" Lesley informs Bethan.

"Hello Bethan" the little man offers, coming over to the bed to sit down.

"May I?" he asks gesturing towards the bed.

"Of course" nods Bethan.

Aleister hitches up his navy chalk stripe trousers and perches neatly beside Bethan.

"OK" he says opening a glossy black briefcase with a short combination of numbers on a gold dial.

"Have they been treating you well?" Aleister enquires, turning his body toward his new client. He is obviously attempting to smile warmly, but he looks tired and the world-weariness he wears at his foundations betrays any lighter expression painted on top.

"Yes, everyone's treated me very well. Though I did ask if I needed a solicitor earlier and was told that I didn't."

"Yes that's an oversight from the police in our favour" Aleister's pale blue, birdlike eyes appear to twinkle at this.

"Why am I here?" Bethan asks tentatively.

"Well first you were treated as a witness and you gave a statement."

"Yes" agrees Bethan.

"Then, the police saw the incident from some CCTV taken from some apartments, literally right next to the car Mr Gadsall was in."

"Saw the incident?"

"Yes. They recovered evidence quickly and they know that you didn't commit the actual murder. Now they need to check to see if you were complicit in anyway with the murder or the planning of it to see if they can charge you with soliciting in murder under a joint enterprise."

"But they have charged me with that haven't they?" Bethan feels so confused.

"No, they've arrested you as they had grounds for suspicion that you might be involved somehow in the murder. Now that you have been arrested, they will detain you here whilst they investigate. But they can only keep you here for so long. Then they must either charge you for a crime or release you."

"But I haven't done anything" Bethan says indignantly, her sadness turning to anger.

"Indeed. But don't worry, there are things we can do" Aleister replies, attempting to inject a jollier tone into proceedings.

"What are the police doing now?" asks Bethan.

"Well, they will search your home and computer, check your internet history to see if there is any mention of a plan. They can detain you without charge for twenty four hours, though in cases linked with murder, they can apply to increase this to up to ninety six."

"They can't do all that can they?" Bethan asks.

"I'm afraid they can" Aleister replies bleakly.

CHAPTER 27

"Gov, that was Vivek from tech" Dan informs Nicky after speaking on the phone. "They can find no mention at all of any plans to hurt Pete Gadsall on any of Bethan's devices, the iPhone we seized, and a Dell laptop at her house. There was also an Amazon Fire seven, which is obviously her son's. The only mention of him is directly to him through text messaging and on an online dating app and Bethan also mentions him to her friend Fiona in a text message. Pretty innocent stuff."

The feeling in the room of dissipating tension is palpable, like air seeping out of a too full balloon. Nicky and Dan feel better now that there is no trace of a plan on Bethan's phone or computer.

Neither detective feels comfortable being in Bethan's house whilst a search is going on to find any evidence of possible collusion here. Neither of them thought there would be any such evidence on Bethan's electronic devices or in her home and felt badly for intruding into her personal life. At least now they can rule out evidence having been found of a plot to murder or hurt Pete on Bethan's phone or computer. Both Nicky and Dan are fairly certain that the four officers searching for evidence room by room here in Bethan's home will not find any either.

Nicky stands in the large downstairs area of Bethan's maisonette, which is both a kitchen and dining room. The other rooms are reached by going upstairs, the living room, bathroom, two bedrooms and loft.

A collection of drawings on the wall above the dining table

catch Nicky's eye. Child like drawings, presumably drawn by Dylan. Some brightly coloured, wonderfully expressive dinosaurs breathing fire and giving each other high fives. It warms her heart to see how valued and cherished tokens of a child's imagination are in this home.

"That's a relief" smiles Nicky. "Not unexpected, but a relief. The sooner she can get back to normal now, the better."

Nicky turns her attention to a stack of reports on the table of students from the secondary school where Bethan works. The detailed descriptions of the kids and what Bethan thinks would help their situations causes Nicky to smile sadly. Poor Bethan.

"Definitely" Dan smiles too. Neither of them thought there would be any evidence that Bethan colluded in Pete's murder, but they had to make absolutely sure. People have surprised them both too many times.

CHAPTER 28

Bethan awakens. She can hear the delicate, hushed chirping of songbirds somewhere nearby. That strange feeling of waking up in a bed alien to your own envelops her. Then, in what feels like no time at all, it comes flooding back to her. The scratchy charcoal blanket she requested last night, and the plastic of the pillow sticking to her face are not from a hotel room or a friend's house. She spent the night here in this police cell.

Bethan feels oddly vulnerable without a device by which to measure time. She lays there, clutching the blanket to herself like a shield for what seems like three quarters of an hour. A hatch in the top third of the cell door spills open, turning it's face at a forty five degree angle to form a table.

"Morning. Breakfast" Lesley's voice good naturedly calls through the opening.

Bethan watches as Lesley's be-ringed fingers carefully pass through a white plastic tray.

Before Bethan has a chance to call out 'good morning' in return, or thank her, the briskly efficient Lesley has gone.

Bethan tentatively makes her way over to the hatch. A thin white plastic bowl containing what looks like cornflakes with milk, and a white, polystyrene cup of dark looking tea, peer back at her.

Bethan carries the tray over to the bed and puts it down carefully. She sits down beside it and begins to eat the cereal with the red plastic spoon which Lesley has provided.

It tastes nice. Sweet, crunchy and not mushy. Bethan drinks the tea and sets the tray down onto the floor. She curls up in the corner of the bed, wrapping the blanket around her. She remembers Aleister Asquith telling her that it would be highly unlikely that she would be able to get a shower. He also said not to graffiti the walls as this would just result in her getting charged with criminal damage, and to be as polite and cooperative to the police as possible.

Bethan thinks to herself. She wonders how Dylan is, and her mum. What exactly DS Sheppard told her mum. She thinks of her work and if this spell with the law could impede it somehow. Would the school still employ her after this? Would she be able to get private work? All work with children now requires a DBS check. Is this classed as a criminal record? She hasn't actually done anything. Surely they'll realise that. Won't they?

She picks up the leaflet she was given yesterday by Lesley. It has some how helped Bethan to cope with all of this by fiddling with this leaflet. Rather like one of those anxiety cube toys or a stress ball from the nineties. Bethan feels the comfort of the narrow cone shape she has fashioned it into. She unfurls it and begins to roll it into a tight cylinder. She glanced briefly at the leaflet's contents last night. It said that toilet paper, sanitary items and toothbrushes could be requested.

Bethan sighs, discards the leaflet onto the foot of the bed, closes her eyes and leans the weight of her head back against the wall.

CHAPTER 29

"You're being released" Aleister Asquith informs me.

"Oh" my eyebrows raise in relieved delight. I sit up straighter on the cell bed.

"The police could find no evidence against you."

"Released on bail?"

"No, no. No bail conditions as the police don't believe there will be any evidence to obtain against you in time."

"OK, that's great" replies Bethan with tired relief.

"The custody sergeant will be along shortly."

"Right, OK, well thanks for everything Aleister" Bethan feels a little awkward as she likes Aleister and he's done a lot to help her, but pleasant though he is, he doesn't seem as though he engages in unnecessary comradery with other people.

He allows Bethan a firm handshake, nods, then picks up his briefcase and quickly and neatly walks out of the cell.

Bethan smiles, at least she can go home now and part of this nightmare is over.

***

Bethan is handed back her belongings together with a leaflet entitled 'Information For Victims of Crime'.

"You're in luck" declares Lesley Bird the custody sergeant. "PC

Chambers can drive you home."

"Oh" and a grateful smile is all Bethan can manage to reply. Lesley is actually a lovely, sweet soul and it must be hard doing this job.

DS Sheppard is waiting by the reception desk next to Lesley. He smiles kindly at Bethan and hands her two cream coloured business cards. "Hi Bethan, if you think of anything at all you need to talk to us about, these are direct contact details for DI Cosgrove and myself. Contact us immediately if you feel you need to. PC Chambers will drive you home now."

"OK" says Bethan, taking the cards.

PC Chambers is a dark haired, nice looking younger man of around twenty. He smiles at her and indicates towards the door.

Bethan opens the door to her house, a wonderful feeling of safe familiarity washing over her. Although she isn't the first person to do this since that dreadful night, as the police have conducted a search here, they appear to have left it in reasonably good condition. The only evidence of them having been here is some slight disarray. Bethan feels so relieved at having been allowed to go home that she doesn't even feel her usual compulsion to tidy up, she's just so grateful to be back.
Bethan takes off her coat and leaves it, with her bag on the table. She should call her mum. Shirley will be worried sick and Bethan is anxious to hear how Dylan is, she's missed him terribly. Bethan calls her mum from her iPhone which she's so pleased to have back. Just having a phone enables a person to have a wonderful amount of freedom.

"Bethan, are you alright? The police phoned me!" Shirley's voice is filled with worry.

"Hi, yes I'm fine. Are you? I'm so sorry if you were worried."

"I was, you were arrested for murder?"

"No, of course I wasn't arrested for murder Mum. It's a long story but I'm safely at home now."

"Oh good, what a relief."

"Is Dylan alright?"

"Yes, he's fine, he's been showing me how to build a tree house on his gadget. I've told him to turn it off now though."

"That's good." Bethan smiles as she thinks of Dylan and the games he so enjoys.

"So you're sure you're OK?" Shirley's voice sounds uncertain.

"Yes. Well, no. Something happened and the police needed to check I didn't have anything to do with it. Someone hurt a man I know. Knew." *Loved. Love* Bethan wants dearly to add.

"Oh no! Is he alright?"

"Um m, not really." Bethan can feel tears stinging the backs of her eyes. She swallows them back. "Could you possibly have Dylan for me for a bit? Not long, just.."

"Just till you feel better. Of course darling. Do you need anything?" Shirley's kindness and understanding swells Bethan's heart. Having such a helpful, emphatic mum makes a bad situation so much more tolerable.

"No" Bethan answers silently. *Just Pete*, she thinks.

CHAPTER 30

Bethan slumps down onto the stairs. Tears spill down her face. She's been so caught up in worrying if the police were going to wrongly convict her, if she'd languish in that cell, or worse – one in prison for years that she'd put the enormity of what happened to poor Pete to one side.

She suddenly feels so selfish. The kindest, dearest person she could ever have met has been murdered and she was just relieved that people didn't think it was her. And that her mum and son are alright, when Pete's family will never see him again.

Oh God, Pete. Bethan's heart physically hurts as tears of raw sorrow stream down her face. She'll never again kiss or touch that wonderful man. Never again hear him laugh.

Bethan's whole body, whole spirit aches for Pete. How can she go back to how she was before she met him now? He's come along and made her love him. And now he's gone.

Was he in pain? Was he scared? Did he call for her to help? Questions taunt Bethan's mind until she can no longer think.

Was it a man or a woman? The police wouldn't tell her anything. Oh she should have asked more, not have been so concerned by what what happening to her.

Oh God, was it a group of people? A gang?

Sinister thought after sinister thought tortures Bethan's ravaged mind. It's just the most awful thing she can think of.

She'll never know now. Never know if she and Pete would have had a future together, travelled the world, had more children, laughed and shared silly moments together only the two of them understood.

Bethan feels very tired. Tired and dirty. She needs to have a bath and try to wash some of this nightmare from herself. She pads up the stairs and into the bathroom.

Bethan twists the bath taps on as water rapidly gushes into the tub. She removes her clothing and folds each garment into a neat pile. Trousers, top, items she had selected carefully, excited for her date with Pete only a short time ago, seeming like it happened in a previous lifetime.

Bethan watches dispassionately as the hot water rises. She turns the tap off and climbs into the bath. It's a bit too hot, her skin will be irritated afterwards. There was obviously a time when she'd care. She looks around the room at the familiar items. The candles, the shells, the bubble bath, half full. When she started the bottle, bought it from the shop, took it home and poured the first drops into this bathtub, she'd never heard of Pete. Never knew a charming, easy to laugh, interesting person lived in the same country, not far away. Caught colds, worried about bills, ate and drank too much, lived, loved. Now, with the meniscus just three or four inches down, she's met him, laughed with him, kissed him. Now he's dead, gone. In only three or four inches worth of bubble bath.

Bethan doesn't dry her hair or even comb it through. She just climbs into bed and pulls the duvet over her head, wishing only for the blessed relief of sleep.

CHAPTER 31

You're alone now, just like I was. You're not completely alone, not properly. But you feel that awful questioning don't you? Why you? That sense of despair that the one person who understood you, could see straight into you, not the superficial crap that everyone else chooses to see, because they're too stupid to see anything else, but the real you. Your essence. And they loved it, unconditionally, you didn't have to be scared to let them see because they won't turn their head in disgust. They'll reach out their arms and hold you. And then they're gone and you have only a memory that someone once thought you were alright.

CHAPTER 32

I miss you so much I can't speak. Can't think. Lovely is a silly overused word but it describes you perfectly. You were lovely. Just perfectly lovely. Who could do that to you? Plunge a blade into your soft neck and drag it across? Did they look into your eyes? Your sweet wonderful eyes? Was it difficult for them or did they just get on with their day afterwards? Tick it off a to do list?

I just can't believe it. I will always be changed now, never be quite the same. My life before Pete, and my life after him.

I wish I'd known him longer. We could have been together, lived together, had a baby together. I can't accept that he's been killed. Waiting in his car, probably tapping along to a little tune only he could hear. He did that. Waiting in his car for me. Fucking stupid me.

This is making my head spin. I feel panicked and I genuinely do not know what to do. I think I'd like to talk to someone, a friend. There's no way I can tell Fiona.

I pick up my phone and type out a text message to Andy. I write three or four attempts to explain the situation, yet each sounds sensationalised, ludicrous. I don't really know what to say. In the end I send the one which my natural reserve compels me to settle for.

'Hi, hope you're well. Just wondered if you were about, could do with a friend. X'

I get back into bed and pull the duvet over my head. I don't want a crack of light coming in, I find it taunting. Like the sun has any right to be shining today. I truly don't know what to do with myself. The only thing I want to do is sleep as then I don't have to think about it. I'm scared to close my eyes though as the recollection of discovering that awful line, long on each side but with a zed shape in the middle, like a flash of lightning may be seared into my mind forever.

A tentative knock at the front door jolts me from my solicitude. I'm much more jumpy and easy to frighten than normal, even more so than when I was always worried about Tom and what he might do next.

I open the door to Andy, the look of concern on his face causing fresh tears to spring at my eyes.

"Hey" says Andy. His voice is calming.

He guides me up to the living room and we sit together on the sofa.

"Thanks for coming mate, I really appreciate it" I say, squeezing his hand. He clasps both my hands into his.

"Oh" I suddenly think to myself, "It's not going to get you into trouble with work is it? Coming here straight away like this?"

"What? Oh no" Andy momentarily looks perplexed. As though I'd suggested he should have alerted the African Embassy or something.

"Oh that's good. You're lucky with your work. They're OK about this sort of thing. I phoned the school this morning, I didn't set my alarm so it was a bit late but no one's phoned me back so I think it's OK. I offer a half smile to try to lighten the air but I'm well aware that I'm rambling.

"What's happened Bethan?" Andy asks me calmly.

I take a deep breath, try to compose myself enough to tell him,

I can feel myself shivering and my voice shakes, it's frustrating. I have to keep stopping as my voice catches. Andy sits and listens patiently, never interrupting as I tell him the terrible events of last night.

"Bloody hell" Andy raises his eyebrows in disbelief.

"I just can't believe it. Can you? Round here I mean, in the whole time I've lived here, never once have I ever.....Oh my God!" I gasp, my eyes enlarging as a truly horrendous thought occurs to me. "You don't think it was him do you, Tom? He's had it in for me ever since that date I had with him." My voice quickens as I run with the idea "he put horrible pictures on my fence and I'm sure he's been here in my house moving stuff about!"

"In your house, moving stuff about? Did you tell the police that hun?"

"No. I didn't think to. Oh it all adds up, it's got to be him!" I look at Andy who enfolds me in his arms.

"I would definitely tell them about him. He's been acting like a complete wanker for ages now."

"Yes. I will, I'll tell them" I say, worried that if it was indeed Tom, this nightmare may be only just beginning.

CHAPTER 33

Nicky and Dan hear Dr Aan Visser humming as they walk along the corridor towards the post mortem room of the mortuary. A strong smell of disinfectant becomes increasingly more pungent. It always makes Nicky feel a bit sick.

The convivial Dutch forensic pathologist often hums Jazz type tunes, counts or talks to himself as he works. Nicky is well aware however, that, quirks aside, Dr Visser's knowledge of his field is second to none and the force are incredibly fortunate to be working with him. Fluent in six languages, and a lecturer at The Royal College Of Pathologists for sixteen years, he is fascinated by the workings of the human body and a deep reverence for his diseased subjects is always apparent.

The tall, broad, middle aged doctor also has a childlike, artless sense of humour and fun. Nicky enjoys seeing his beady eyes twinkling. It's balm to the soul that somebody who works among victims of violent, brutal deaths can retain such wonder for the world and express it with ease.

"Hello DI Cosgrove, DS Sheppard" smiles the doctor as the detectives enter.

"Hi Dr Visser" says Dan.

"Hi Dr Visser, what have we got then?" Nicky says, polite but clipped.

"Well" begins Dr Visser, emerging from behind a steel post mortem table, his pea green gown straining across his corpulent middle. "Cause of death would have been fairly rapid exsanguination as the external jugular vein is severed. However, the wound itself is quite shallow. Both the internal jugular vein, and the external and common carotid arteries have been missed."

Dr Visser looks at both at Nicky and Dan, realising they are both lost.

"Your man bled to death" he offers. "The action of him tipping his head back caused the blood from the severed vein to run down his throat, causing some choking. This is also why there is no external bleeding."

Dr Visser continues, "The cut is much deeper here on the right, then gets much more shallow as it goes towards the left. This is consistent with a right handed person using a small spear point blade initially inserted forcefully, then loosing its depth as it slices along."

Dr Visser mimics this movement. "I am thinking a pen knife?"

"How long would it take him to die in this situation, if no one were around to help?" Dan asks contemplatively.

Dr Visser walks across to the other side of the room towards a row of fridges."Ah it would happen in minutes" he calls back.

***

Dan Sheppard lifts the photo of himself and Jessica skiing in Nendaz in Switzerland. He runs his thumb gently over her beautiful face. Her lovely hair, small features, smattering of freckles she hates but he'd kiss every moment of every day if he could. Nearly a year now since her job in healthcare transferred her to Australia. Did he make the right decision? How many times has he asked himself that to the nearest ten?

Turning down the chance to live with the most beautiful, caring and carefree woman in the world, in a wonderfully warm, sunny climate with better pay and cheaper housing?

Dan had recently passed his Sergeant's exams in the police, and had not long bought this flat, and so he felt it wouldn't be right to emigrate with her. He's pleased for Jess, she's doing what she wants. He'll always love her, who wouldn't?

Dan relishes the opportunity to cook a nice meal. Just pasta with chicken and leeks in a white wine sauce, but he can feel the release, the purging of all the tension and stress as he weighs and assembles the ingredients. It's quite a rarity to have the time and energy for cooking, but Nicky is coming round tonight to discuss the Pete Gadsall case.

The detectives would usually be working around the clock in a murder investigation, being on call at all hours of the day and night. But Dan and Nicky have been able to snatch a couple of hours to have a bite to eat at Dan's place because the investigation seems to have reached a bit of a standstill.

There have been no witnesses coming forward and nobody who was questioned in the door to door questioning in the area knew of anything. It's almost like someone pressed a pause button for the time that the murder took place and then the sleepy little market town of Elmsfield carried on as if nothing had happened. Indeed, were it not for the CCTV footage which Dan and Nicky have clearly seen with their own eyes, it's eerily like the incident never happened at all. It's frustrating not being able to work a case and feel as though you are in limbo, but they are both on call until any new information comes to light.

Dan is glad to catch up with Nicky for a little while. He knows she's been upset in her personal life and finds it difficult to talk about her feelings, but she's obviously hurting. Julia just doesn't understand the pressures of a senior officer in the police. People dismiss Nicky's aloofness as insincerity but Dan sees it for the coping mechanism it is. Nicky's a warm, loving person, she cares passionately about protecting people. She just needs to trust people more, trust that they won't leave her like her Mum and Dad did.

Dan turns the heat down on the hob slightly as he fries up the chicken pieces. The buzzer sounds. Jess never liked the buzzer, said it used to give her a shock. Dan smiles at the thought of her, his heart tightening with longing.

"Hi" Nicky says coming into the flat. Dan likes how she's able to relax a bit and knows she values their friendship enormously.

"Hey, that smells lovely" Nicky says appreciatively, taking off her knee length black trench coat and laying it neatly over an arm of the sofa. She slips off her shoes, courts, though not overly high, Dan still feels, at five foot seven, stunted in comparison. It seems lots of women are taller than him, but he's OK with it.

"Next time you come over, I'll stew some lamb in cardamom and turmeric, I've not had a chance to use that new tagine yet."

"That'd be lovely" smiles Nicky, her olive green eyes looking tired.

"How's things with Julia?" Dan asks tentatively.

Nicky sighs and puffs out her cheeks "Much the same really" she shrugs.

"So what do you think about Pete Gadsall then?" Dan pours Nicky a glass of white wine and one for himself.

"I think it was personal. I know it was personal. It may even be a professional hit, it was so clean."

"That person on CCTV, you think he could be a professional? Then on who's behalf was it?"

"I don't know" Nicky swills the wine around in her glass in thought. "Pete didn't seem to have any capital, no previous, one serious ex partner with no animosity."

"No animosity that we know of" remarks Dan.

"True. It's odd that no one has come forward. It happened opposite a Sainsbury's. Just so odd" Nicky looks confused.

"It's like time froze when it happened. No one has come forward and we can't get a positive I.D on the person on the CCTV." Dan shrugs, he hates feeling so useless.

"My heart goes out to Bethan, imagine going on a date with somebody, nipping over to the shops and then returning to find they'd been murdered?"

CHAPTER 34

"Bethan?" Shirley says kindly, her face a mask of worry. "What on earth's been going on?"

Bethan smiles at the sight of her mum at the door. She gestures for her to come in. Shirley opens her arms and Bethan relishes the comforting refuge they offer. She can feel Shirley's grip tightening with worry and safeguarding.

"Let's sit down, you want a coffee?" asks Bethan going through to the kitchen.

"If you're making one love" replies Shirley, her voice pregnant with worry.

Bethan busies herself in the kitchen, it's small square form a welcome familiarity within this awful, nonsensical ocean which constantly threatens to drown her.

"So you know that guy I was seeing?" Bethan silently acknowledges how sad it is that referring to Pete in the past tense has now become second nature.

"Do you want Columbian or just normal?" Bethan simply doesn't know how to begin, pussy-foot around or just rip it off quickly like a plaster?

"Whatever you're having" her mum replies patiently.

"Well" Bethan sighs, closes her eyes and leans on the counter. She thought the arbitrary act of preparing the drinks would make it easier to formulate the words to tell her mother of the horrendous incident. She feels awful as she knows it'll upset

Shirley, and she wants to protect her from that. But Shirley would worry more if she didn't know, if this were Dylan, Bethan would want to know exactly what had happened, however awful.

Bethan sighs deeply. "We went on a date, it was wonderful. Perfect." She has stopped spooning coffee into the mugs and focuses on a small granule on the counter top which she rolls between her finger and thumb. She is grateful her mum is not pushing to learn more before Bethan is ready to tell her.

"We stopped near here, as I wanted to dart into Sainsbury's quickly. Just to get some milk. He waited for me in the car. I went into Sainsbury's, When I got back to the car.." Bethan looks at the older woman, she's so small, it'd be like delivering a punch with one of those comedy boxing gloves on a spring. Could her mum take it?

"When I returned to the car, he was dead" Bethan looks straight at her mum.

"Oh my goodness, no! Oh you poor thing, that's awful" Shirley reaches out her arms to hold her daughter.

"Was it a heart attack? I've read about this, healthy youngsters can have them just like that."

"No. He was murdered" Bethan sees her mother's eyes widen in horror and in them, the reflection of herself in despair.

Bethan and her mum sit on the sofa, both trying to digest the terrible news. Her mother sits forward, hands clasped around her coffee mug, looking off into the distance and Bethan feels awful for hurting her.

"He was so funny, he really taught me to loosen up" Bethan muses, to herself or to her mum, she's not sure. Shirley sighs and shakes her head, utterly incredulous as is Bethan.

Bethan jumps as her phone rings. Angela called this morning and said she could take the rest of the week off so it may be her calling to see how Bethan is, Angela is actually deeply kind hearted, people can surprise you positively as well Bethan thinks to herself. Its a nice thought, something to cling to.

The number calling is unfamiliar, though it has a local dialling code.

"Hello?" answers Bethan.

"Oh hello, is that Miss Bethan Archer?"

"Yes" replies Bethan, looking over at her mum who is wearing a questioning look.

"I'm Millie Heart from 'The Elmsfield and District Gazette. I'm so sorry to hear about your recent experience. How are you holding up?" The voice sounds as though it's testing the ground perhaps, rather than genuinely wanting to learn the answer.

"Um m, well OK. Shocked."

"Yes I can imagine, how awful for you Bethan. Do you mind if I call you Bethan?"

"No" replies Bethan quietly.

"Well we're running a piece on the incident. As you can imagine, something of this magnitude happening in Elmsfield is highly unusual and there has also been interest from the nationals. You could tell people how it made you feel, get it off your chest, it'd probably be very therapeutic, not to mention pretty lucrative."

"Um m, no I don't think so. I'm still trying to get my head round it and I can't tell you how I feel as I honestly don't know."

"That's perfectly understandable Bethan, anyone would be exactly the same. Sounds like you're dealing with it really admirably I must say."

"Oh, thank you."

"Could I get your side of the story?"

"It's not a story, it's true"

"Of course it is, I'm so sorry Bethan I didn't mean it like that. Can I get your side of events? Give you a voice?"

"Um m no, I wouldn't know what to say. I don't think I could."

"I think you could, you're obviously very strong. No one else can say what you saw can they?"

"Well no but I think I'd just like to keep it private if I can. I can't profit from Pete's death."

"Very admirable and I totally understand. You could always give the money to a charity. Victims of crime or something."

"No, I really couldn't"

"People will be asking you anyway as there has been a great deal of interest."

"Yes, I'm sure, I mean nothing like this has ever happened before to my knowledge."

"Exactly, and that's why people are so shocked and will want to hear your side of things, in your own words."

"Well like I say, I don't really know..."

The phone is snatched out of Bethan's hand by the small whirlwind that is her mum. Shirley speaks clearly and directly into the phone, the register of her voice adopting a more refined, somewhat haughtier timbre than usual, like a butler from another time.

"She's not interested OK? Now bugger off!" and then in a softer tone, "Bloody vultures, I thought this might happen."

CHAPTER 35

Bethan misses her kind, thoughtful, son tremendously. Misses talking to him, cuddling him, the funny, perceptive things he says. She hopes he's alright and not worried about her. The thought of causing him any worry, allowing the smooth, creamy skin of his little forehead to pucker in torment making her feel worse, if that's possible.

Bethan's stomach rumbles noisily. It occurs to her that she hasn't eaten anything for a day and a half. Just a few cups of tea, more from the need for something to do than something to drink. She just feels so very tired, depleted, bereft.

This whole nightmare has made time stand still, but the thing is it can't. She has a job waiting for her to return to, a son who needs her. Wonderful as Shirley is, Dylan can't live with her in limbo while his mum unravels like a knitted scarf nearby.

No, Bethan knows she needs to get herself and Dylan settled and secure as they were before all this, however hard that might be. Dylan needs the familiarity of routine.

Her phone trills on the bedside table. Bethan spent the night re-reading messages Pete had sent her. As though words he wrote might bring back a piece of him. If only that could be true.

It's Fiona. Bethan presses 'accept', glad to hear from her friend.

"Oh my God, hun, I've just heard! Are you alright, no of course you're not, stupid question, oh my God!" Bethan's heart is pierced by her dear friend's anguish.

"Hi mate, it's OK" Bethan's strong desire to protect people from any kind of hurt needing to assuage Fiona's worry, particularly as she's due to give birth any day now.

"How are you? What happened? I can't believe it."

Bethan sighs, smiles bittersweetly. Fiona's words are those of herself only hours ago.

***

The house is quiet without John. Fiona knows she should be savouring this time before the baby comes. Napping, watching Netflix and pampering herself. Yet she just can't relax, can't really get comfy in bed, whichever way she lays, dreadful heartburn prevents her relaxing.

How terrible for poor Bethan. She helps people, is a wonderful Mum, daughter and friend. Dates one guy who turns out to be some kind of twisted stalker and then another guy who gets murdered. You couldn't make it up. If it were a soap opera people would say it was unrealistic. Fiona sighs, she doesn't know what to make of anything at the moment. She hauls herself up from the sofa and takes herself into the kitchen to make some lunch. She's not hungry, just going through the motions to try to feel normal, anchor herself to something real.

She's glad she decided to stay with John. She does love him. She doesn't really know Brian and the concept of excitement, by definition, can't really last. She'll speak to John about going away more and doing fun, quirky activities together. She knows he'll be amenable and it's not like they don't have the money. Maybe they could take up a sport together, something not too taxing, meet new people. Fiona smiles faintly, it's a nice idea, but she can't focus on anything besides Bethan at the moment. Poor, poor Bethan. She'll go and see her this afternoon, take her some flowers.

A knock at the door startles Fiona. One of those confident, chipper, old fashioned type knocks. Tuneful. Who can that be? Fiona heads towards the door, one hand on the small of her back, it's really been hurting lately.

"Hello" says a chirpy older lady smiling widely. Fiona looks blankly back at her, should she know her from somewhere or has the lady mistaken her for somebody else? Oh no, don't say this is going to be a drama as well. Fiona really isn't in the mood for an unannounced visit from one of those healthcare people who visit you at home, they mean incredibly well, just always sound so patronising, referring to you as "Mum". Fiona can't help but be quite impressed that this lady still does that at her age.

"Janet Bowman, your curtains and baby bits?" the lady offers in a mild, kind voice, still smiling broadly.

"Oh sorry I completely forgot!" Fiona's eyes widen in alarm, her eyebrows shooting up into the depths of her fringe. "Oh I'm so sorry" Fiona tells the lady, feeling awful.

"It's quite alright, we all forget things now and again" the lady, Janet continues to smile warmly and genuinely.

"I can always come another time if you like love?"

Relief seeps through Fiona's tired body, this lady's lovely but she really doesn't want company.

Then she hesitates. She looks at Janet, although Fiona's first reaction was to gratefully accept and reschedule, it might do her good to take her mind off things.

"No, you're here now, come in" Fiona replies meeting the woman's cheerful smile with one of her own, it feels good.

"If you're sure love?"

"Absolutely, thanks for coming."

"What a beautiful home. Is this baby your first love?" Janet asks entering the hallway.

"Yes it is."

"How are you feeling in yourself?"

Fiona shrugs, "Tired, excited, just had enough of the backache and heartburn now"

"Oh, I know that feeling" offers Janet.

Fiona leads Janet into the kitchen. "Can I get you a tea or coffee? I've got the most gorgeous fabric" Fiona smiles.

"Let me make you one love" says Janet, and with a gentle insistence, takes the kettle from Fiona and fills it. "You go and sit down."

"Oh thank you, I can't get onto those bar stools now, so I'll see you in the living room? It's just next door. Thank you Janet, it's ever so sweet of you."

"No problem love, cups in here?" Janet enquires, pointing to a cupboard.

"Fiona sits in the living room on one of the velvet sofas. She feels the warm energy of having someone like a Nan fussing around her. Fiona never had a Nan, only an Auntie, who was never particularly friendly to her or her sister. Some adults just don't like children, and children are usually wary of them in return. Janet's presence in her home feels nice and she suddenly wishes it were thirty years ago and she and this kindly old lady could bake ginger bread men together.

"Here we are" says Janet bringing in two steaming mugs of tea.

"Oh this is nice love, did you design it yourself?"

"Yes" answers Fiona beaming proudly.

Luckily, the swatch of fabric is still in Fiona's bag from when she showed Bethan. So much has happened since then it feels like a lifetime ago. Dear Bethan, Fiona feels a tear come to her eye.

"Hey" says Janet gently, her voice full with concern. "Have you had a lot on your mind?"

"Oh God, sorry, I'm so embarrassed" Fiona looks down at her mug as tears fall freely down her cheeks.

"Not at all." Janet doesn't appear at all ill at ease at having a stranger crying in front of her, just genuinely wanting to help. Her kindness causes Fiona to let everything out. And so Fiona tells Janet about John and Brian, and what happened to poor Pete.

Janet squeezes Fiona's knee and hushes her, it really does feel like having a Nan.

"I'm so sorry to offload onto you like that Janet, I'd never normally do that."

"Well it's not every day your best friend's boyfriend gets killed is it?" offers Janet, gently imploring Fiona to see the logic in her considerate way.

"No" concedes Fiona. She feels better for having told someone. Someone objective who doesn't know anyone involved. Fiona can't remember when she was this open with a veritable stranger before, if ever. But it feels OK, and precious little has done lately.

"Have you always made things from fabric?" Fiona sniffs, wanting to take her mind off things by immersing herself in another person's world.

"No, a very long time ago, I worked in a jewellers, and then I got a job at St Anne's, the children's home. Secretarial work. I was there thirty odd years until they closed twelve years ago. I've always liked making things with fabric though, and I do it now to keep my hand in, keeps me young." Janet shrugs, "I don't like gardening and I'm allergic to cats, so I thought it'd suit me. Plus the extra money means I can do things".

"That's great. Oh my friend stayed at St Anne's."

"Oh what's your friend's name?"

"It's Bethan, Bethan Archer."

"Oh the one who found Pete dead, bless her, poor thing that'll stay with her."

"Yes. Why did the home close, was it lack of funding?"

The older lady exhales a world weary sigh.

"Well I mean after it happened, nothing was ever the same. Patricia, that's the boss, managed to keep it out of the papers and quite quiet you know. But everyone felt different after that."

Janet shivers slightly, has a troubled look in her eye, at odds to the wide smile of before.

"I mean, yes I heard things" she sighs, "it was different back then love, very different. Now I'm offloading onto you look," her chirpiness is back but Fiona senses it conceals a deep hurt.

"What happened? What did they keep out of the papers?"

"Oh love I shouldn't say, I'm sorry."

"No it's OK, I'm interested."

Janet sighs, "There were these two little lads. Brothers. It was evil. They came to us covered in bruises, cigarette burns, you wouldn't believe it. Their Mum used to lock them outside all night, must have been awful for them. One of them was older, he was quite boisterous and Patricia kept him in a room on his own. I thought it was cruel after what he'd been through with being outside on his own you know, but it wasn't my place to say anything so, Lord forgive me I didn't. Odd given her job but I don't really think she liked children. Particularly not little boys. She thought that was the best way to deal with it. Seems unbelievable now."

"The younger boy, Tristan, he was quiet, silent almost. Broke my heart, I say looking back now, I'd have questioned things but it was different then."

Janet looks straight at Fiona, her eyes deep pools of pain and regret. Fiona pats Janet's arm, offering comfort the older women gave her only moments ago.

Janet looks into the distance, touches a small, gold crucifix around her neck which Fiona hadn't previously noticed. "The poor little mite jumped out the window and killed himself."

"No!" Fiona covers her mouth in horror.

"He was lovely Tristan, they both were. Gorgeous looking boys, really bright red copper hair."

"What was the brother's name?" Fiona asks.

"Sean. His name was Sean."

CHAPTER 36

It's a sunny day today, the sun caressing everything with it's healing rays. It doesn't feel as abrasive as it would have done days ago, it's like the universe is somehow urging me to begin a new. I still feel breakable, horribly exposed. But today I'm going to collect Dylan from my mum's and try and get settled back as we were. He needs it and so do I. Happy son, happy mum. I'll probably feel like an actress unused to a roll at first, encased in an ill fitting suit of armour. But it's better than living in this limbo world. I think it's what Pete would have wanted.

I busy myself with some dusting and hoovering. It usually annoys me how those black mould spores appear around the window panes when I've not wiped them for a few days, but now its a welcome sight, offering me something to do to prepare my home for a normal life. It seems like something somebody practical would set about doing.

I might do a bit of shopping today, go down to the Tesco store on the Millbank. They've got some quirky gift shops there, I might buy something for my mum.

A sharp knock at the door startles me. I hope this jumpiness that's taken hold of me lately soon wears off, it's exhausting.

I open the door to a troubled looking Fiona.

"Hi, how are you?" I enquire, hugging her. It's so nice to see her. It feels like she's come at just the right time, when I'm gearing up to plait myself together again.

"Hi darling, not too bad" she smiles but still wears a look of slight unease.

Fiona and I sit in my living room clutching mugs of hot chocolate.

"How are you?" she asks me.

"I don't really know" I answer, truthfully. "The police were very nice to me" I add, shrugging, "I got the impression that the lady, Nicky really didn't want to arrest me because she believed in me."

I sense Fiona is elsewhere and wants to tell me what's on her mind, and so I gently enquire.

"Bit of a strange thing happened earlier, the lady who's making my curtains and the things for Tamsin's room, she's lovely, her names Janet. Well she came round."

"Oh right" I say, receptively.

"Yeah, I forgot she was coming but like I say she was so easy to talk to, we got chatting. She told me she used to work at St Anne's children's home doing secretarial work."

"OK" I offer, wondering what it is she's getting to.

"I hope you don't mind, but I told her you'd stayed there."

"Not at all, it was years ago and it was fine. I just missed my Mum that was all" I reply sunnily, hoping to put her mind at ease if divulging that I stayed there is what's obviously bothering her. Compared to what's been happening lately, that's the least of my worries.

"Well she said there were these brothers who came there. The younger one, called Tristan jumped out of a window bless him and killed himself."

"Oh no, that's hideous! Oh poor thing" I say, horrified.

"I know, its terrible. Well the older brother was in a room on his own to calm him down as he was boisterous."

"Seems a bit Draconian, he probably really needed his brother. You hear things like this, I mean now we know that victims of trauma require..."

"Bethan" Fiona says, placing a hand on mine to halt my chatter.

"His name was Sean and both the brothers had bright red copper hair. Well I was just thinking, when we were in Pizza Express that time, that waitress called Andy Sean, do you remember? She looked certain that was his name didn't she. And he has bright red copper hair as well." Fiona looks pointedly at me, eyes widening to bring home the point.

"So you think Andy is the older brother?" I ask slowly, disbelief contorting my face.

"Yeah maybe."

"But he grew up in London."

"Maybe he's just saying that."

Suddenly I feel a bit irritated. Fiona has never liked Andy much and I've always felt she feels threatened that I have another close friend besides her which I just find petty and immature. But I keep my cool, the last thing I want to do is fall out with Fiona on top of everything else.

"OK, well I appreciate you telling me hun. It's far fetched but everything seems to have been lately. Yes it is odd. I'll have a think about it."

CHAPTER 37

I need to get out of the house, this is all too much. I feel like my head is going to explode, the safe cocoon of my house feels quite stifling. For the last couple of months, I've not been able to shake the sensation of walking arm in arm with a feeling of abject vulnerability. As though I'm on edge all the time, waiting for the next thing to happen. The thing which might finally cause me to shatter into a thousand pieces, like a crystal vase tottering on the brim of a shelf.

It feels wonderfully renewing to inhale some fresh air. Air that isn't tainted with sadness and disappointment. I feel a bit self aware, as though I shouldn't be trying to piece my life back together again. I'm sure it's because I haven't left the house in days and have become a bit stagnant, and so I shake the feeling off.

It's nice to see the bustle of our little town. The cafes and shops are busy and it feels for a delicious moment, as though I've gone back in time. Before this nightmare began.

I shiver a little and push my hands into my pockets. As I make my way towards the end of the high street, it curves around into a more quiet, residential area. I remember this area well. St Helen's Road. It's where a friend of mine from school used to live. I remember her Mum was always singing, and I loved the feeling of joyous energy the house used to exude.

St Helen's Road is quite a climb and I'm suddenly annoyed at how unfit I've become. I pause for a moment by a lamppost to catch my breath. Perhaps Dylan and I could get a little dog, take it out for walks, I could get a bit fitter and it'd be something the two of us could do together.

The top of the hill gives way to a cul de sac called Orchard Close. I smile at fond memories of myself and various school friends riding around on our bikes and playing hide and seek in the shrubby area at the end which leads onto a large field.

Reaching the shrubby area which seemed so expansive when I was young and so tiny now, I arrive at a pathway, through which I have walked, run, and cycled countless times as a youngster. People feel sorry for me when they hear I've spent time in care, but I have lovely memories of school, friends and seemingly endless summer holidays buying ice pops from the garage and playing in the park.

At the end of the pathway, I arrive at the field. The familiar sight of the walkway and benches around the perimeter makes me smile. I'm not kidding myself, I did used to feel things other than dread.

There are some kids playing football, some Mums nattering on a bench, babies blissfully sleeping in prams by their side. I see an old gentleman, impeccably dressed, bending to crumble some bread for some eagerly awaiting pigeons. Their dark blue grey bodies hopping from foot to foot like a tennis player anticipating a serve.

I come to the end of the field which forks into three directions. The first leads to a woodland area, the second to a beautiful estate of new houses, and the third over onto a further field in which the long closed St Anne's Children's Home stands. Something makes me select the third option. Maybe Fiona mentioning the home earlier.

This second field has a different feel about it to the other one. One of neglect, almost seediness. No one comes here, I've always noticed that. If there ever were people around here, one would assume they were up to no good. This field contains no youngsters playing football, no Mums stopping for a natter, no-body feeding the pigeons. Indeed, no pigeons, as if wildlife can also feel that heaviness permeating the air, as if urging all living things to stay back.

I head towards the building. It looks so unloved. Smashed or boarded up windows, broken fencing and graffiti. Each time I stayed here, I remember it being very clean and well main-tained. I wonder how many kids stayed here over the years? Such a shame that time has been so cruel to it. I notice a large sign advertising new build homes which the dilapidated old building is at some point going to made into.

As I head toward the end of this field which circles back onto the other side of the high street, I see a figure standing, apparently taking in the building as I had a moment ago. Still like a statue, hands in pockets, feet slightly apart, as though rooted to the ground. I don't know why or how, but instinctively, I know it's Andy.

CHAPTER 38

"Hi" I say, trying for a blend of cautious and friendly.

Andy doesn't turn round. "Hi" he replies cordially.

"Are you alright?" I ask, pulling my coat around me, the temperature seems to have dipped.

Andy sighs deeply. I don't know whether to comfort him or stay back, nothing I say or do feels natural any more.

"Do you know what it's like to try and get to sleep with your arm broken in three places?" Andy asks me this matter of factly, as though asking if I've ever been to America or something.

"No" I reply in a chocked, almost inaudible whisper.

"Andy, did you stay here as a child?" I ask tentatively.

"I did indeed." His reply is filled with false chirpiness.

"Andy, did you have a younger brother?"

Andy sighs again, the weary, bitter sigh of somebody completely let down by the world.

"Do you remember him?" Andy asks, still with his back to me.

"Andy" I walk towards him but he turns around swiftly, eyes of pure hatred boring into me like lasers.

"Do. You. Remember. Him?" Andy asks me again, every word over enunciated and sounding as though he's trying not to lose his temper. A temper I never knew he possessed.

I can feel my jaws clenching together, a funny feeling creeps up my insides and settles uncomfortably in my stomach.

"Was his name Tristan? Fiona said today that she met someone who worked here and they told her about what happened. I'm so sorry Andy."

"I'll ask you again, do you remember him?"

"No, I honestly don't. I stayed here three times when I was a kid. I can't remember how long it was each time. My mum and I haven't discussed it. It was months or weeks at a time I guess. I think I made some friends but I can't remember Tristan. I remember just missing my mum is all. I'm sorry." I feel as though I've got the answer wrong and disappointed Andy.

"He loved you you know" Andy seems to stare without actually focusing on anything as though absorbed in the wilderness of memory.

"Andy, I honestly.."

"And when you left to go back to your happy home, to a Mum who wanted you, he felt completely alone."

Andy focuses on me again, he looks utterly broken.

"That fucking bitch locked me in a room on my own so I couldn't look after him. Did you know that?"

"That's awful, that should never have happened to you. But I was a child, I only knew a few of the kids and a couple of members of staff there. I didn't know anyone else who was there and I had no idea stuff like that was going on."

"You really don't remember Tristan? Sweet, kind, loving? The best little person who ever lived? Loved everyone despite everything that'd been done to him every day of his little life?"

Andy lets out a noise that sounds like pure, undiluted anguish.

He swipes his hand across his nose quickly, then in a more measured tone, continues.

"I heard years later that he used to follow you around."

"Follow me around? I remember a girl, Kerry-Jane, and another girl, Alison I think. I don't actually remember any boys to be honest."

"She hated boys, she told us that, that rhyme saying they're made of snips and snails and puppy dog's tails."

"Bloody hell, right when you needed someone to make you feel safe and settled, you had to put up with that?" I'm incredulous, I truly am.

It had never occurred to me before, but now I think about it, I don't remember any boys, certainly not older ones.....

"Oh God" I feel my legs give way from under me, as though I'm trying to stand on an octopus's legs. Realisation hitting me like a thunderbolt.

"Oh God, Twisty?" I whisper the name from long ago, every fibre of my being wishing for it not to be true.

Andy stares at me, utterly disenchanted. Any vestige of kinship we ever had evaporated.

I can hear my voice, it sounds small and dismembered as I reach into the darkest crevices of my memory bank, horrified with understanding.

I go to an old oak tree I've just noticed, my legs won't take me and I need to support myself, but I can feel myself sinking before I can grasp it.

"I couldn't pronounce 'Tristan' so I called him Twisty. He called me Betha. Oh God, yes he was adorable, I didn't realise, Andy I was just a child."

"He loved you and you left him."

I capsize to a kneeling position. The ground feels never ending, as though any minute I'll feel the nickel at the centre of the earth.

"He was lovely, you're right he was a sweet heart. Andy I had no idea."

Another juggernaut suddenly strikes me.

"You killed Pete, it was you." I look up at Andy as bewildered realisation dawns on me.

"I wanted you to know how it feels! Losing someone you love, needlessly, because of someone else's selfish actions! I couldn't bring myself to do it to Dylan!"

"The mention of my son's name fills me with anger, I try to get up but the next thing I know I hear a scream, animalistic, primal and Andy surging towards me. The speed of time is altered, it seems somehow slower, drawn out. I feel an intense pain in my neck, at the side, right I think. I open my mouth to scream, raise my hand to shield my neck, it feels tacky. I feel myself falling, falling backwards. And then everything is black.

CHAPTER 39

"Fiona? It's Shirley here, Bethan's mum. Sorry I hope you don't mind love, I didn't know who to call, so I looked you up on Facebook and saw your number. Dylan showed me how to do it."

"Oh, hello Shirley" Fiona doesn't think she's ever had a chance to talk properly with her friend's mother before. She wiggles into the sofa, attempts to gain some support from the backrest.

"I'm sorry to call you like this Fiona, I know it's late and you're probably trying to have your dinner, but Bethan hasn't come home and I'm a bit worried."

"Oh" Fiona's sole attention is now with Shirley.

"Yeah, I've tried calling her mobile quite a few times, but there's no answer. I know you two see a lot of each other and I just wondered if she'd mentioned to you that she was going out somewhere?"

"No, she hasn't told me she was going anywhere" replies Fiona, the tingle of dread making itself felt.

"You don't think she'd have gone on another date and forgotten to tell anyone do you?"

"I shouldn't think so after everything that's happened" remarks Fiona dryly.

"Maybe she's just gone out and is fine" Shirley says, though she can't disguise the worry in her voice.

Fiona collects her thoughts and forces herself to think what the best course of action is.

"Shirley, would you mind if I came over, are you at Bethan's house?"

"No, I called her a few times and there was no answer, so I thought she may have lost her phone. So I came over to see if she was in, I had to bring Dylan of course because I'm on my own. Though I didn't want to upset him if she wasn't in. Poor thing's had a lot to deal with lately."

"Yes he has" Fiona agrees with the voice of the protective grandparent. "Would you mind if I came to yours? It might be nothing, but I have an idea."

"Of course, it's number three, Evergreen Walk. Near the vets?"

"Give me your postcode, I'll whack it in my sat nav."

Fiona then informs John that she needs to pop out, puts on her coat, and, leaving her slippers on as it takes her too long to put on her boots, leaves the house.

An outdoor light awakens as Fiona ascends the steps onto the short pathway to Shirley's front door. It's one of those doors with a misty glass, diamond shaped pane in the top third with a curtain on the other side. Almost immediately, Fiona sees Shirley push aside the curtain, and the evident relief on her face when she sees Fiona standing there.

"Hi Fiona, thanks for coming love, its probably nothing but Bethan does normally tell me if she's going out. Not that I'm her keeper of course, but she told me earlier she was going to come by and collect Dylan this evening, so that the two of them can get back to how they were before, well you know."

Fiona nods her understanding.

Shirley continues, her fingers entwined whilst the two thumbs wheel around one another. It's an ingenuous little movement, a neat, confined habit evolved over many years. Though also, an obvious sign of Shirley's inner turmoil.

"Anyway, she never came and I'd be putting him to bed soon normally."

Fiona thinks for a moment, inhaling a deep breath through her nose. She doesn't wish to worry Shirley unduly, but inadvertently doing so may be necessary in order to help find Bethan.

"The thing is, now this could honestly be absolutely nothing, but earlier I got talking to a lady who used to work at St Anne's. She said there was a boy there with bright red hair called Sean."

"Right" Shirley says softly, wide eyed at what Fiona may reveal.

"Well for some reason it struck a chord with me and I thought that boy could be Bethan's friend Andy. We were out having dinner recently and the waitress called Andy, Sean. And he's got red hair."

"OK, I've heard her mention Andy" Shirley's eyes look tired and confused.

"Do you think, Bethan being Bethan, that she went to his house to talk to him about it or met up with him somewhere?"

"Well, supposing she did, why didn't she let me know? She knew Dylan was expecting her to come round here, and it meant a lot to her as well, I could tell. I mean I know the police might have to question her again and then obviously Dylan would come to me again, but in the meantime, she said she wanted things to be as stable as possible for Dylan and for him to come home with her sooner rather than later." Shirley explains earnestly, her bewilderment tugging at Fiona's heart.

"The thing is, if he changed his name, he might not want anyone to know he'd stayed there, I mean, he'd never told Bethan, even though St Anne's is in her home town."

"You think he doesn't want anyone to know and then Bethan will try and talk to him about it, how he feels and that?"

"She does try to save everyone bless her" Fiona points out softly.

"Yeah, true. Well even if he didn't want to talk about it, why would she be with him now? Maybe he got really upset and she felt she needed to stay with him and has lost her phone?" Shirley's eyes appear far away, as though lost in the task of mulling over possibilities.

"That's reasonable. The other thing I was thinking, and again, it could be nothing, is Tom." Fiona looks straight at Shirley, hating having to cause her friend's Mother more worry.

"Tom, who's that?" asks Shirley warily.

"That first guy she went out with a couple of times. Do you remember? They went to the pub in town, things started off well but then Bethan didn't want to see him again."

"Oh yes I remember" Shirley looks a little alarmed, clearly on edge.

"Shall we go and sit down, I'm so sorry love, I've forgotten my manners." Shirley looks dismayed that the two women have been standing in the hallway by the staircase and not sitting in the living room. Shirley leads Fiona into an adjacent lounge.

Fiona eases herself down onto a dun coloured settee upon which, a clay coloured waffle throw is strewn.

"Thank you" smiles Fiona.

"Sorry I didn't think to say before" Shirley says, obviously embarrassed.

"Please don't worry Shirley, it's honestly no problem" Fiona's kind smile seems to cause Shirley to relax and, as she sits down in a matching armchair opposite, her features noticeably unknot.

"So this Tom" says Shirley.

"Yeah, well I know they went out a couple of times and it didn't work out. But then after that, I remember Bethan mentioning that a file she's been working on had gone missing."

"She thought Tom had taken it?"

"I think it was the timing that freaked her out. It happened just after Tom said something really nasty on their second date."

"Oh? What was that?"

Fiona sighs, intensely wishing she didn't have to further upset Shirley.

"He said that Bethan was wearing a necklace on their date just so that other men would look at her breasts." Fiona hangs her head, she can't stand the thought of any distress on Shirley's sweet face.

"What? But why would.."

"That's exactly what I said, and exactly what Bethan said too. That's why she didn't want to pursue things after that" Fiona shakes her head, empathising in this poor lady's disbelief.

"Why would wearing a necklace make people do that anyway?" dubiety settling all over Shirley.

"Exactly. I suppose he thought it'd drawn attention to them. I honestly don't know" Fiona shrugs, being able to offer no explanation.

"Anyway, I got the impression that Bethan seemed a bit scared of him after that, with him living nearby" Fiona tells Shirley.

"This Tom chap?"

"Yep. It seemed like the wind had been knocked out of her sails after that, for quite a few weeks actually."

Shirley's teeth visibly clench a little, she looks angry that her lovely daughter spent her energy on somebody so richly undeserving of her. Fiona completely understands this feeling.

There's a beat of silence whilst the two women think.

"So what are we going to do?" Shirley asks quietly, an earnest look in her eye, hopeful, as though Fiona has the answer.

Fiona is scared that she does.

CHAPTER 40

"Well, I've tried calling and like you say, there's no answer. So I think, if she's still not home yet, we should call the police."

Shirley's eyes widen in alarm.

"That lady who's working on the case of Pete being killed. Bethan said she liked her and thought that she believed in her. I'm pretty sure her name was Nicky."

"OK, do we call the local station and ask to speak to her?"

"Yes, lets do that." Fiona takes her phone from her coat pocket and Googles the contact number of the local police force. Shaking her hair out of the way, she then puts the phone to her ear.

Shirley sits opposite looking overwrought. Her thumbs continuing their futile journey round and round each other.

A crisp female voice answers.

"Good evening, Kent Police, can I help you?"

"Hello. Yes, I was hoping you could. A friend of mine recently witnessed a crime, well the aftermath of one. She hasn't come home and was expected a while ago at her mum's house but hasn't arrived yet."

"OK, what's your friend's name?"

"Bethan Archer."

"Is she under eighteen?"

"No."

"Does she have any serious medical requirements?"

"No."

"Does she have any mental health problems?"

"No. I don't think so."

"Has she ever gone missing before?"

"No, I don't think so, just one minute.." Fiona covers the mouth piece and asks Shirley if Fiona has ever gone missing before. Shirley answers that Bethan has not. Fiona returns to the phone conversation.

"Hi, sorry about that, I was just checking with Bethan's mum, no Bethan hasn't ever gone missing before."

"OK, that's fine. Does Bethan have any learning difficulties?

"No."

"OK, can I take your details?"

"Yes, It's Mrs. Fiona. Bradshaw."

"OK, and who are you in relation to Bethan?"

"I'm a close friend."

"Right, so she hasn't come home?"

"No. Or to her mother's house either. The thing is, there's a police detective who is working on the case in which Bethan is a witness. She knows Bethan and I could be wrong but I think Bethan not coming home and the case could possibly be linked."

"OK, what is the detective's name?"

"I only know that her name is Nicky as I heard Bethan mentioning her earlier."

"When was this?"

"This morning, around eleven. Could you put me in contact with Nicky please."

"I'll ask her to call you as soon as possible OK Mrs Bradshaw? Which number could she reach you on?"

Fiona gives the operator her mobile number and thanks her.

"She's going to ask Nicky to call me A.S.A.P" Fiona tells a concerned looking Shirley.

"OK, lets hold tight till she calls. I'll not put Dylan to bed yet, I'll just check, make sure he's happy upstairs."

"OK" smiles Fiona, trying not to look as though serious worry has just started to seep into her.

Fiona inhales deeply trying to stay calm. She's not generally given to panic, but this situation is making her feel very uneasy.

She absorbs the cosiness of the room. A black fireplace with one of those 'living flames' style fires sits in the centre of the facing wall. It's hypnotic flames licking up to form creatures and images. A wicker shelving unit holds lush looking green house plants and small pots of brightly coloured flowers cradled in Delft china saucers. At the front of the room, a large, curved bay window is concealed by silky beige and silver striped eyelet curtains. Under different circumstances, Fiona thinks she'd enjoy falling asleep with a good book in this room, waking up to it's snugness.

Shirley comes back into the lounge and sits down on an armchair opposite Fiona.

"He's happy as Larry up there, playing on his computer thing and reading." Shirley looks relived about this.

On the arm of the sofa, Fiona's phone begins to ring displaying an unfamiliar number.

"That'll be Nicky" says Fiona, noticing Shirley's thumbs twirling faster and more furiously than before.

CHAPTER 41

"Hello?" Fiona answers the phone, hoping it is indeed Nicky who has called.

"Fiona Bradshaw? It's DI Nicky Cosgrove. You say Bethan hasn't arrived home?"

"No she hasn't. The thing is, she had arranged to come over to her mum Shirley's house this evening to collect Dylan and get him back into his routine with her again. She knows you might need to speak to her again of course, but she felt she needed to have Dylan with her again. They're very close."

"Of course, children need routine and he might have been wondering if his mum was alright. So it's actually a very good idea."

"Exactly. Anyway, Bethan said she'd come to Shirley's to collect Dylan and take him home. She hasn't come yet."

"What time was she expected?"

Fiona asks Shirley this who replies that Bethan said she'd come over at around six. It's now nearly quarter to ten.

"Six. I mean, I know it's only a few hours, but it's really not like Bethan to forget and go somewhere else instead. In fact, no, she'd never do something like that. Dylan's her world and she was really looking forward to seeing him. We thought with everything that'd been going on, something might have happened."

"No, you were right to call me, I'm glad you did. Who's 'we'? You said "We thought"?"

"Shirley and I. I came over to Shirley's house when she phoned me to tell me that Bethan hadn't come to get Dylan as planned."

"Would it be OK with Shirley if I come round too?"

"um m, yeah I would have thought so, I'll ask her."

Fiona turns to Shirley, "Would it be OK if Nicky comes round?"

Shirley nods emphatically, "Of course, we want to find Bethan."

Fiona returns to Nicky on the phone, "She says yes absolutely."

"OK, if you could give me the address, I'll be over shortly."

***

Shirley answers the door to a very tall, elegant lady wearing a knee length dark coat, and a slightly shorter, quite muscular looking guy who smiles warmly at her. They both show their respective police ID's to Shirley.

"Shirley Archer? I'm DI Nicky Cosgrove, Fiona Bradshaw phoned me from here around fifteen minutes ago."

"Yes, of course, come in."

"This is DS Dan Sheppard. Thank you" both Nicky and Dan make their way into Shirley's house.

"Hi Shirley" says the man, DS Dan Sheppard. He has a warm kindness about him, as though he'd be easy to talk to.

Shirley leads the two detectives into her lounge. Nicky walks over to the sofa and sits down next to Fiona.

"Hi Fiona, DI Nicky Cosgrove."

"Thanks for coming so quickly" replies Fiona.

"Hi Fiona, DS Dan Sheppard." Dan offers his hand out to Fiona whilst he makes his way to the furthest armchair, perhaps noticing that it looks as though it isn't used as much, and that Shirley might prefer to sit in the one nearer to the sofa, which, with the cushions askew, and the throw falling down slightly on the back rest, looks to have accommodated her recently.

Fiona shakes his hand. Shirley lowers herself down into the arm chair nearer the sofa.

"Do either of you have any idea where Bethan could be at all?" Nicky looks both at Shirley and Fiona.

"No, I honestly don't, that's why I called Fiona." Shirley appears pale and anxious. Fiona wants to hug her.

"That was good thinking calling Fiona" offers Nicky. Dan nods in agreement and smiles reassuringly at Shirley.

"Well, I had a couple of ideas" offers Fiona.

"OK, that's great. Can you tell me what they were?" Nicky gently enquires.

"Well, after everything that's been happening in Bethan's life lately" Fiona shrugs, "Things which may have seemed fairly innocuous before take on new significance don't they."

"Yes they can do" agrees Nicky.

"Well Bethan dated a guy before Pete called Tom. They only went out a couple of times because he really upset her with something he said on one of the dates. After that, Bethan seemed a bit shaken up, for a few weeks afterwards actually. It was me who encouraged her to go out with someone else to try to take her mind off Tom. I think he'd really scared her."

"Do you know Tom's surname?" Dan asks Fiona whilst writing something down on a small, spiral bound notepad.

"I don't I'm afraid" replies Fiona shrugging in a futile gesture.

Katherine Clare

"OK, what were your other ideas Fiona?" Nicky asks.

"Well, this morning I had an appointment with a dressmaker to come to my house and discuss making things for my baby's room. She's a lovely lady, really friendly. Her name's Janet. Anyway, she told me that she used to work at St Anne's children's home."

Fiona glances over at Shirley. Hearing somebody tell two police officers that your daughter spent time in a children's home when they were small cannot be easy for anyone. Fiona feels awful about it, and worse too that she's doing it in Shirley's home. In a way, Fiona wishes she never mentioned what Janet told her to Bethan. Fiona feels like a common gossip and is worried she's embarrassed Shirley. Moreover, it may have something to do with Bethan not coming home.

Shirley seems to sense Fiona's discomfort and offers her a kind, understanding smile. Fiona notices there is the slightest glimmer of tears in her eyes.

"I couldn't cope, just couldn't seem to do anything. I missed her every day." Shirley shrugs, and an overwhelming sense of the sadness and regret she must have carried over the years hangs heavily in the room. It permeates the walls, curtains and the room's occupants, who each wonder for a moment what Shirley must have been through. Fiona's hand travels to the precious mound she's been carrying and nurturing. The thought of her being completely alone and having to give Tamsin up to a care home almost stopping her heart. She feels a swell of emotion and takes a deep breath, trying to remain calm and concentrate on the task at hand – finding Bethan.

"Are you alright?" Nicky asks Fiona kindly.

"Yes" replies Fiona smiling with a rather forced cheer.

"So Janet said that there were two brothers who came to St

Anne's" Fiona continues. "One of them, the older brother was called Sean. I know it's probably nothing, but my husband John and I were out having a meal at Pizza Express a while ago, I can't quite remember when it was. It was an evening, quite recently. Bethan and her son Dylan were there, and also, a friend of Bethan's called Andy. The thing is, when the waitress saw him, she greeted him like an old friend, and called him Sean. He seemed quite embarrassed. He also has bright red copper hair like Janet said the brothers did. I mean, lots of people have red hair but to specifically describe it as bright red copper? Andy's hair is an unusual red, kind of coppery. I know, it seems daft now, I just thought there might be something in it."

"So the waitress called Bethan's friend Andy, Sean?" Dan asks Fiona.

"Yes, he told her he didn't know who she meant but she seemed really sure."

"Bethan's friend Andy, do you know his surname?" Dan asks.

"No, sorry." Fiona replies.

"Right so this Tom lives locally?" Nicky asks Fiona.

"Yes, I'm certain Bethan said he did."

"OK, and what about her friend Andy?"

"I honestly don't know anything about him. I do seem to recall Bethan telling me that Andy grew up in London but I don't know anything else."

"OK, right, we'll look into this, do some digging around and call you as soon as we learn anything OK. Obviously if Bethan does come back, could you ring me immediately?" Nicky takes out a handful of business cards from her coat pocket and passes one to Fiona. She then gets up and goes over to Shirley, passing her one as well.

"This is my direct number. Call me if you think of anything at all that could help."

"Yes of course" says Shirley opening the front door for Nicky and Dan.

"Bye Shirley, we'll be in touch" Dan smiles his warm, reassuring smile again. Shirley however, feels very far away from being re-assured.

CHAPTER 42

That was some fun I hadn't bargained for, that idiot Tom coming into your life. You feeling on edge like that and questioning everything. I don't know what he said or did but it really upset you. Faking that letter from him was easy, I can imagine the tone a man like him would have struck.

My dear little brother, sweetest kid you'd ever know. Because you did know him didn't you? I wonder if you would have ever thought of him again if I hadn't reminded you of him, that he lived.

CHAPTER 43

"We don't have any records of any kids who stayed at the home" Nicky tells Dan.

The trilling of Dan's phone cuts trough the air of tension in Nicky's office.

"Hi Tina, what have you got?" Dan answers, his customary warm, friendly tone laced with misgiving.

"OK, right, yes exactly" Dan makes a noise of agreement with the person who has phoned him.

"OK Tina, that's brilliant, thanks for being so quick about it, bye."

"What gives?" Nicky asks Dan.

"Right, that was Tina. She's located twenty six 'Seans' over the age of eighteen in Elmsfield and it's neighbouring villages, and has emailed their full names and addresses to me now." Dan informs Nicky of this whilst logging into his email account.

Nicky and Dan look at the concise, neatly prepared list of 'Seans' spelt both 'Sean' and 'Shaun' along with their addresses which Tina has swiftly sent over. Both detectives are acutely aware that they need to act fast as Bethan could possibly be in danger. Somehow, some why, somebody is angry with her.

"OK, we don't know what this guy Sean slash Andy's surname is, where he lives, works, or in fact anything about him. We need to look for a connection to Bethan with each of these men." Nicky takes a deep breath, "lets get stuck in".

Dan looks at the first of the 'Seans' on the list.

"Right, Sean Lewis, flat 1, Magnolia Way, works for Western Electronics and has done for, let's see, twelve years. All that time he's lived with his wife Emily Lewis and their three children, one of whom is only three. I don't think it's him."

"What if his name really is Andy and that waitress genuinely made a mistake. What if this Andy slash Sean has nothing to do with Bethan not coming home. I'm going to get a list of all the 'Toms' in the area and find the one Bethan went out with. We know he upset her and she's been scared because of him."

"OK, I'll do the 'Seans', you do the 'Toms'" declares Dan.

***

"So I know it's a long shot, but it may be worth checking out." Fiona stands in the kitchen her arms around John. John has turned the Aga off, halting the meal he was preparing for them both and is holding Fiona in his arms, realising her need to talk.

"OK darling, you think maybe Bethan went to the old children's home?"

"Well most likely she went to his house, her friend Andy."

"Who you think is Sean. But is it possible she might have met up with this Tom character?"

"No, Bethan would never meet up with Tom. I know her John, she wants to save everyone, help them. If she found out that her friend Andy did stay at St Anne's and has changed his name, she'll want to tell him she understands and wants to be there for him. That's what Bethan's like, she thinks with her heart."

"OK. But Bethan knows you'd be worried, and her mum would be too, and Dylan. She'd let someone know if she'd gone to see Andy or anyone she was meeting wouldn't she?"

"Well yes I'd always have said so. Oh John, if I'd never told her about what Janet said, Bethan would be safe now, I just know it's got something to do with that."

John sighs, hating to see his wife in such distress. "I mean, I honestly think she could have met up with this Tom, who's a much nastier piece of work than a friend of hers who just happened to change his name through personal reasons. Maybe he just didn't like it. People change their names all the time."

"No. I know Bethan, I'm sure she went to tell Andy what I told her. I think Andy got upset, she's with him and can't contact anyone for some reason."

"Do you think she's in a place where she can't get any reception?"

"Yes it's possible. I hadn't thought of that."

"Maybe Bethan is with someone else or maybe she's on her own and Andy has no idea about any of this."

"Yes that's possible, of course it is. But John, I saw Andy's face that evening when that lady, Kelly called him Sean. Don't you remember how he reacted? He looked really embarrassed and keen to change the subject."

"But he was with you, who is very much Bethan's friend and maybe he felt a bit nervous, shy, awkward. Maybe he just doesn't like attention on him, some people really don't."

John holds Fiona tighter to him.

"I feel like you cuddling us resembles a little kid trying to put its arms round an oak tree."

"Don't be daft darling." John kisses Fiona on the forehead, then adds to the bump, "We'll be seeing you soon wont we Tamsin?"

John looks at Fiona, "Honestly darling, try and calm down.

You've told the police, they know the best way to act. That's all you can do. Try and take your mind off it now, you can't be stressing yourself out."

"John. I just know she went to meet Andy. With only good intentions. To try to help him, I don't know. But I do know Bethan."

And something in Fiona's eyes, an imploring need for him to help her compels John to do so.

"Right OK, lets drive round there and have a look. Just to put your mind at rest."

CHAPTER 44

"Luckily it's not too dark" remarks John, turning off the ignition.

Fiona opens her door, shivers slightly in the chill night air. John's right, they are lucky it isn't pitch dark like it was only weeks ago. Now the evenings are drawing out and it stays much lighter well into the night.

Two street lamps illuminate the deserted car park by the top field where the dilapidated ruin of St Anne's stands. Fiona supposes that's thanks to the adjacent collection of new build houses that there are now street lights here, giving the area a more occupied feel.

Fiona looks over at the old building. It's clearly visible from here in the car park. She imagines a little Bethan peeping out of one of the upstairs windows. What must it have been like living there? Bethan has always maintained that it was fine. But now with the thought that Andy may be Sean and didn't want anyone to know about his past when he stayed here, like a redundant limb one can never amputate, the building seems to evoke a much more insidious feeling.

Fiona is certain Bethan went to meet Andy, and furthermore, that Andy is Sean. Why didn't he want anyone to know? What happened back then? She's tried researching the home online but there are no records. Nothing at all.

Fiona sighs with frustration, this is futile. Bethan may have gone to Andy's house and Fiona has no idea where that is. Bethan may have met Andy somewhere completely different. Somewhere significant. An outing the kids from the home went to or something. Fiona's mind is running away with her, spinning with ideas born of worry. She needs to focus.

"Well it doesn't look like there's anyone here darling" shrugs John. "Lets go over and have a look."

The car park leads on to a footpath which in turn leads to the field. Between the two are a row of wooden bollards, long ago kicked over, yet still stubbornly trying to retain their positions as sentinels of an institution.

Fiona and John instinctively tighten their grip on one another's hands. This field has an eerie feel to it. It suddenly occurs to Fiona that she's glad John is here. In fact, she wouldn't want to be doing this with anyone else. The three members of her little family off on a quest to look for their friend. Fiona smiles faintly for a moment, then reality hits her, they're in a dark field walking to an old abandoned children's home to see if her friend has met up with someone who could have hurt her. If it were not so creepy, it'd be madness.

Both Fiona and John pick up on the palpable sense of abandonment and emptiness, the nearer they get to the carcass of the old children's home.

"Bethan!" Fiona calls into they night. Only utter silence answers back

"Bethan!" calls John, his voice sounding hollow as it travels into the abyss.

"Bethan!" Fiona calls again. "Andy!" she tries, again to complete noiselessness.

"There doesn't appear to be anyone in the actual building, we cant really enter, it'd be trespassing" says John, thinking aloud.

"Lets walk round the front bit. I'm genuinely surprised there's no one here, kids smoking or something."

John and Fiona walk the length of the building towards what would once have been its entrance. This is where Shirley must have stood watching her daughter leave her thinks Fiona mournfully.

If there is anyone in the building, they are being incredibly still and quiet. Maybe sleeping? The night is so still and doesn't have the sense of having been disturbed. The seal of dust motes and atmosphere not having been broken by the presence of another being.

"Well it was worth a try" shrugs Fiona.

"Exactly. Lets walk round the back of the building back to the car, then we know we've circled the whole thing."

"Good idea." Fiona puts her arm around John and makes to set of around to the other side of the building.

"Fiona!" John gasps in a loud whisper.

"What?" Replies a shocked Fiona on full alert.

"Over there by that tree, look."

A dark shape becomes apparent as Fiona looks towards a sprawling, elderly tree.

The shape at the foot of the tree seems odd, It doesn't appear to be a natural part of the landscape like a log or a fallen branch.

Fiona and John approach the shape which as they draw near is obviously the silhouette of a person lying on the grass.

"Oh my God! Bethan!" Fiona cries.

CHAPTER 45

Absolute horror courses through Fiona as she takes in her friend's broken body on the ground. Bethan's long, toffee coloured hair covers her face, one of her legs is stretched out, the other twisted at an awkward angel.

"I'll call an ambulance darling, its alright" says John, trying to remain calm for the sake of Fiona.

Fiona feels as though she's in some sort of hellish dream world. She can hear John speaking to somebody on the phone about needing an ambulance and a woman being hurt. His voice sounds detached, far away. Oh God, is Bethan dead?

Out of nowhere, a searing pain travels the length of Fiona's body causing her to cry out. She looks around for somewhere to sit but there's nowhere. She makes her way to the tree by Bethan's body. She can't look at her friend, it's too awful. But she needs to lean on the tree for the support it would offer her. As soon as the pain has finished its trajectory, it seems to disappear, as though she merely imagined it and it never actually happened. Just then, another fierce, ripping pain steels through her body. Fiona closes her eyes tightly, grinds her teeth together and tries to keep calm.

Fiona feels a bit breathless, unable to inhale a deep, satisfying breath, only little, shallow ones. Suddenly, she feels her jeans soak with wetness. But it isn't the warm wetness of urine.

"John, I think my waters may have broken" Fiona tells John in a small, anxious voice.

John speaks back into the phone, "we'll need to make that two ambulances, my wife is abut to go into labour!"

CHAPTER 46

"It's OK, are you in any pain?" John asks his wife.

"No, it seems to have stopped for a minute."

"OK, that's good, they know where we are, they said they'd be here within half an hour."

"OK."

"Lets just try and wait calmly", John says trying to sound reassuring but feeling anything but calm. What if Bethan is dead? She hasn't moved since they found her. Did that mean someone killed her? No, she must have fainted and passed out. Maybe she hasn't been eating properly because of everything that's happened. Maybe she just went for a walk to clear her head and felt dizzy suddenly. Stress can do all sorts of things to people.

John crouches down next to Bethan. She looks very still, it's hard to determine if she is breathing or not.

"Bethan" John very gently shakes Bethan's shoulder to try to rouse her. She doesn't move. He reaches his hand down and carefully gathers the hair hanging down like a curtain in front of her face. Her eyes are closed. John carefully and surreptitiously tries to feel for a pulse in Bethan's neck. He feels the cold metal of an earring as he presses down softly towards her jaw bone. His fingers touch something. Crumbly, dry, then it begins to feel like jelly, a half liquid. He knows instantly it is blood. He doesn't want to scare Fiona so carries on trying to deliver a calming front.

"Can you feel a pulse?" Fiona asks wide eyed, obviously worried he'll say no.

"Not sure, how are you doing darling?" John answers, trying for a casual tone of voice.

"Yes I think I'm starting to feel something now. Do you think Bethan's OK?"

"She'll be in the best possible hands very soon."

"Yes that's true, that's good. Yes I can really start to feel something now."

"OK" replies John smiling, whilst simultaneously wishing the ambulances would hurry up.

If it were just Fiona, he and she could wait in the car park where it'd be easier for the ambulances to park and assist her. But John knows Fiona will not leave her friend's side and so the paramedics must make their way over the field in order to locate them. They wouldn't be able to drive the ambulances through the field because of the mature trees surrounding it on the other side. They should be here soon, not long now and both women will be looked after.

John goes over to Fiona who has her eyes closed and is breathing in deeply through her nose, something they taught her to do in the early stages of contractions at the antenatal classes.
He puts his arm around her, feels her shivering slightly.

"I'm quite scared, is it going to really hurt?" Fiona asks, resting her head in the crook of John's neck.

"Nah shouldn't think so" replies John in a jokey voice. They both laugh, it feels good for a second or two.

Just then, relief swamps through John like a river as the yellow beams of torches can be seen in the distance, coming towards them.

CHAPTER 47

"Oh I forgot", Fiona tells John, she looks a little panicked.

"Call Shirley, Bethan's mum and tell her we've found Bethan and that she's being looked after."

It's clear that the contractions are beginning to arrive thick and fast now as Fiona grits her teeth and speaks through a pained sounding breath. It hurts John enormously to see his wife in such pain, he wishes there were something more he could do to help her.

"Call Nicky, the detective finding out about Pete" Fiona places her hands on her thighs, tries to breath through another early contraction.

"Her card, she gave me a card with her direct number on it. Said to call her if we saw Bethan. It's in my coat pocket" Fiona grits her teeth again and makes a low, animal like noise as another early contraction rips through her body.

"Call them and tell them." She says in a breathy voice, obviously trying to fight against the pain.

"I will, don't worry about it." John feels inside the pocket of Fiona's coat and sure enough, locates a business card. He calls the number on the card, sees Fiona suppressing a scream against the pain coursing through her, the contractions are getting heavier and slightly closer together. The torches are getting nearer.

"DI Cosgrove?" A voice answers.

"Hi, it's John Bradshaw here, Fiona's husband. We've found Bethan, she's been hurt but an ambulance is here right now. Fiona is going into labour right now as well so I've got ambulances for both of them. They're here now."

"Where are you John?"

"On the field by St Anne's Children's centre. The old home that closed. Fiona thought Bethan may have come here and she was right."

"You found Bethan there, by St Anne's?"

"Yes in the field by St Anne's. Nicky, I've got to go, the ambulance people are here. Fiona needs me."

"Yes of course, thank you for letting me know John."

"Oh! Also, could you phone Shirley, Bethan's mum and let her know we found Bethan but she's in the best hands now with the ambulance people?"

"Yes of course, I'll tell her right away, you be with Fiona. Thank you John."

"OK."

John ends the call just as four people wearing dark green overalls and heavy boots come into view. They are carrying bags of medical equipment.

"Hi I'm John, this is my wife Fiona. She's in the early stages of contractions, they're getting quicker and stronger" John informs the people, then turns to indicate the crumpled figure under the tree, "This is our friend Bethan. We don't know what's happened to her but she's hurt, we've been here about an hour and a half and she hasn't moved at all in that time."

John wants to give as much detail to the ambulance crew as possible but doesn't want to worry Fiona, so he omits the part about feeling the dried blood on Bethan's neck when he attempted to locate a pulse.

"The reason we're here is we were looking for Bethan, we thought she might have come here you see. The police know she's been found here and been taken to hospital."

"OK" says a woman of medium hight, dark hair pulled back into a clip, as a tall, slim young man rushes over to Bethan's side along with a shortish red headed young woman who applies an oxygen mask to Bethan's mouth, carefully and deftly manipulating the elastic over her head without moving her neck.

The dark haired woman and a tall, grey haired and neatly bearded man hurry over to Fiona, helping her across the field to where the ambulance is presumably parked.

The young man and woman assisting Bethan unfold a trolley bed upon which they work together to lift Bethan's weight and set her down. The young woman unfolds a forest green coloured blanket from one of the canvas bags the group have carried and wraps it around Bethan's body.

Bethan still hasn't moved and her eyes are still closed. John can hear Fiona's voice urgently asking if Bethan will be alright between noises and gasps of pain whilst the paramedics calmly tell her they're doing everything they can.

John hurries alongside Fiona, Bethan and the four paramedics. One of them, the man with the grey hair is speaking on a phone telling somebody about Bethan's injuries. John can't quite make out exactly what the man is saying, everything is so surreal and dreamlike, as though it's all happening under a large body of water, like the ocean.

CHAPTER 48

I can hear faint murmurings of chatter and laughter. I feel warm, pleasantly so. I open my eyes, slowly take in my surroundings.

I'm in a hospital bed, there is a curtain with teddy bears on three quarters drawn around my designated area. I can hear gentle coughing very close by. Somebody in the bay next to me?

I look down and see that I'm covered in three white waffle blankets. Of the type babies used to have when I was young. I'm wearing one of those gowns. It amuses me that my first concern is if they've tied the ribbons up at the back or not and do I need to worry if I need to get up and use the loo, will my backside be on show to all and sundry? I find myself throwing back my head with raucous laughter. How absurd that with everything I've been through – I don't even know exactly what that is or how I ended up here, that that should be my first worry. In a way it's refreshing, mooring myself to normal worries and vanities and nothing more. As I would have done before all of this began.

I see a lady walking past looking down at a clipboard.

"Excuse me" I say in a soft, croaky voice. It hurts a bit to speak, my throat feels sore, as though there's something lodged inside it which won't move.

"Hello" replies the lady smiling widely. She comes over to me.

"I wondered when you were going to join us" she says cheerfully. She has exceptionally long eyelashes and I find myself wondering if they are the ones you can stick on yourself or the individual ones which a beauty therapist applies.

"I'm Dr Jardeen" the lady informs me.

"How long have I been here Dr Jardeen? And how did I get here? Is my mum alright?"

"You arrived in the early hours of this morning, it is now nearly three o'clock in the afternoon.
When you came in, you had a shallow laceration to your throat right here."

Dr Jardeen brings her right hand up to her throat to show me. I do the same and feel the soft fabric of a dressing.

"The wound was superficial, but when you fell, you really banged your head and that is why we had to monitor you. Your mum came earlier, I sent her home and told her I'll let her know when you were awake. Would you like me to do that?"

"Yes, yes please."

Dr Jardeen smiles widely again and pats my hand.

She walks around the side of my bay and I'm aware of her rich, African accent, perhaps Nigerian, talking to somebody. I like Dr Jardeen's voice. It's smooth and soothing. It'd be good for late night radio. I hear her sternly tell the other person to leave at once if I start to look tired and I feel a rush of love for her protectiveness. The voice which answers is also female, though I cant quite place it.

"Hi Bethan, how are you?" DI Nicky Cosgrove enters my bay from behind the mostly drawn curtain.

"OK I think. What happened? I remember talking to Andy and then, then nothing. I can't remember anything else."

"Can I sit down Bethan?" Nicky asks, gesturing to a light blue, plastic cushioned, wooden arm chair next to my bed.

"Yes, of course."

"Thank you." Nicky comes over and sits herself down into the chair, crossing her legs.

"DS Sheppard and I have been speaking to your friend Andy, or Sean Bridger, his real name."

"Is he OK? Poor Andy, Sean. I had no idea about Tristan, I told him that."

"He's a very troubled person."

"It's not his fault, we can't imagine what he's been through" Bethan states fervently, her face a mask of painful empathy for her friend.

"No, I know. He's been through some awful things, him and his brother."

"Yes. I had no idea about any of that" Bethan adds, her eyes wide with horror.

"No one did. The home did everything to cover it up, so it would never reach the papers. Anyway, Sean admitted to attacking you Bethan, causing actual bodily harm, which is a criminal offence. The wound itself turned out to be of little damage, it was the fall which worried the medical staff."

"Almost like he didn't actually want to hurt me, just needed someone to blame" Bethan whispers, almost to herself, a far, far away look in her eyes.

"Yes, that's most likely" Nicky nods.

"Would you like to press charges against Sean Bridger, Bethan?"

"No, absolutely not, he's been through enough. He must have had post traumatic stress disorder for years, decades."

"That's big of you to say." Nicky smiles at Bethan.

Nicky appears to think for a moment, gearing up to tell Bethan something difficult.

"Bethan, Sean has been taken to a medium secure mental health unit. It's a residential centre which has a therapeutic environment to help patients get better at its heart. He'll be comfortable and looked after there."

Bethan squeezes her eyes shut, tears seep through them and run slowly down her face.

"He never meant to hurt anyone" she whispers.

"Probably not" Nicky replies softly.

"Do you think he went for the throat as it represents speech, or the concept of not speaking and keeping quiet? Quick, violent, yet contained, as Andy contained his rage within himself for so long?" Bethan muses to herself, a far away look in her eyes.

"I don't know, maybe" Nicky replies quietly.

"Sorry, I do have a tendency to try to psycho-analyse people" Bethan looks shyly at Nicky. "And sometimes to waffle as well" she adds.

Nicky smiles, she reaches out and takes Bethan's hand. Bethan squeezes Nicky's hand in hers. Shared sorrow for two little boys, so thoroughly failed by the world passing between them, like an electrical current.

Epilogue

Two Months Later.

I gently kiss baby Tamsin's warm, soft head as she snuggles her little self into me. Her dove grey eyes are closed whilst she's lost in the halfway world between sleep and wakefulness. She gurgles a few restless noises, and then settles down into a dreamworld. I breath in her wonderful velvety newness.

"Right, who's for another cup of tea?" Fiona asks heartily as she leaves her living room for the kitchen."

As Fiona passes me, she squeezes my shoulder. I smile, feeling good to be in her house with the people I love most in the world around me.

"Why do babies cry a lot?" Dylan asks, a thoughtful look on his face.

"Well, that's their only way of telling you what they want isn't it" offers John.

"Oh yeah, I suppose so" answers Dylan, looking completely satisfied with this answer, and returning his attention to the game he's been quietly playing on his tablet.

"You OK love?" My mum asks me.

I raise my right hand to my neck, subconsciously touching the faint trace of a pale pink scar which now resides there.

"Yeah fine" I reply, genuinely meaning it.

I stroke little Tamsin's arm, encased in the sleeve of a tiny lemon sleep suit.

I fondly smile at Dylan. He must sense my eyes on him as he briefly looks up from his tablet and smiles back.

The room has that happy, loving feel I've always loved about it. I'm so glad Fiona and John have stayed together. They seem dizzyingly happy, and in love with Tamsin.

I think of Andy, Sean. I hope he's OK and finally being given the help and support he's needed for so long.

I think of my mum and Dylan, the upheaval and worry they've experienced, and how strong they've both been.

I think of my friends, Fiona and John. How they came to my

rescue and how their constant belief in me enabled them to find me lying in the field beneath an old oak tree. How they quickly got me to safety.

I think of Pete. I didn't go to his funeral, but I'll always, always remember him. How he taught me to see the lighter side of life. How his eyes used to twinkle with laughter. How wonderfully loving and kind he was. I think part of me will always love him.

I think of my job trying to help young people when all the time I'd inadvertently abandoned one and spectacularly hurt another.

But most of all, most of all, I think of a frightened little boy with bright red copper hair, the colour of vivid burnt umber.

The End

DEAREST READER

Thank you so, so much for adding *Snips and Snails* to your reading list. The thought of you reading it means the absolute world to me.

Snips and Snails is my debut novel. I am busy working on my next novel now.

I hope you liked the characters I have created. I know Bethan can be a bit preachy but she means well! I felt awful making bad thing after bad thing happen to her.

It was truly heartbreaking to create little Tristan.

I really hope you enjoyed reading *Snips and Snails.*

I have so many other ideas for books, and will be writing many more...

Printed in Great Britain
by Amazon